Kelly looked a
fixed to the da
suddenly blinked

"Don't quit on me now," she muttered, pushing down the panic at the thought of being lost in this maze of twists and turns. The sides were high, giving her the pinched, closed-in feeling that something bad was going to happen.

Stop being silly. You're driving through a storm, that's all.

Her stomach clenched into a tight ball as the storm let loose.

Frantically she yanked the wheel back and forth, to no avail. The water began to fill the canyon as if someone had turned on a giant faucet, causing the car to hydroplane. Willing herself not to scream, she wrenched ineffectively at the wheel. It began to turn in lazy circles until it smacked into a rocky projection and lodged there. Flash flood, of course.

She peered out the window, terrified to see the water rising steadily. It was cresting the bottom of the door and moving fast.

With fingers gone cold she unlocked the driver's door and pushed.

Nothing.

Books by Dana Mentink

Love Inspired Suspense

Killer Cargo
Flashover
Race to Rescue
Endless Night
Betrayal in the Badlands
Turbulence
Buried Truth
Escape from the Badlands

DANA MENTINK

lives in California with her family. Dana and her husband met doing a dinner theater production of *The Velveteen Rabbit*. In college, she competed in national speech and debate tournaments. Besides writing novels, Dana taste-tests for the National Food Lab and freelances for a local newspaper. In addition to her work with Love Inspired Books, she wrote cozy mysteries for Barbour Books. Dana loves feedback from her readers. Contact her at her website, www.danamentink.com.

ESCAPE FROM THE BADLANDS
DANA MENTINK

Love Inspired

If you purchased this book without a cover you should be aware
that this book is stolen property. It was reported as "unsold and
destroyed" to the publisher, and neither the author nor the
publisher has received any payment for this "stripped book."

Recycling programs
for this product may
not exist in your area.

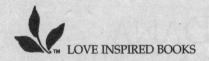

LOVE INSPIRED BOOKS

ISBN-13: 978-0-373-44474-8

ESCAPE FROM THE BADLANDS

Copyright © 2012 by Dana Mentink

All rights reserved. Except for use in any review, the reproduction
or utilization of this work in whole or in part in any form by any
electronic, mechanical or other means, now known or hereafter
invented, including xerography, photocopying and recording, or in
any information storage or retrieval system, is forbidden without
the written permission of the editorial office, Love Inspired Books,
233 Broadway, New York, NY 10279 U.S.A.

This is a work of fiction. Names, characters, places and incidents are
either the product of the author's imagination or are used fictitiously, and
any resemblance to actual persons, living or dead, business establishments,
events or locales is entirely coincidental.

This edition published by arrangement with Love Inspired Books.

® and TM are trademarks of Love Inspired Books, used under license.
Trademarks indicated with ® are registered in the United States Patent
and Trademark Office, the Canadian Trade Marks Office and in other
countries.

www.LoveInspiredBooks.com

Printed in U.S.A.

Dear Reader,

Welcome to Love Inspired!

2012 is a very special year for us. It marks the fifteenth anniversary of Love Inspired Books. Hard to believe that fifteen years ago, we first began publishing our warm and wonderful inspirational romances.

Back in 1997, we offered readers three books a month. Since then we've expanded quite a bit! In addition to the heartwarming contemporary romances of Love Inspired, we have the exciting romantic suspenses of Love Inspired Suspense, and the adventurous historical romances of Love Inspired Historical. Whatever your reading preference, we've got fourteen books a month for you to choose from now!

Throughout the year we'll be celebrating in several different ways. Look for books by bestselling authors who've been writing for us since the beginning, stories by brand-new authors you won't want to miss, special miniseries in all three lines, reissues of top authors, and much, much more.

This is our way of thanking you for reading Love Inspired books. We know our uplifting stories of hope, faith and love touch your hearts as much as they touch ours.

Join us in celebrating fifteen amazing years of inspirational romance!

Blessings,

Melissa Endlich and Tina James

Senior Editors of Love Inspired Books

To Laurie
who is a wonderful editor and a truly splendid sister.

* * *

Therefore, since we have so great a cloud of witnesses surrounding us, let us also lay aside every encumbrance, and the sin which so easily entangles us, and let us run with endurance the race that is set before us, fixing our eyes on Jesus, the author and perfecter of faith, who for the joy set before Him endured the cross, despising the shame, and has sat down at the right hand of the throne of God.
—*Hebrews* 12:1–2

ONE

The site might as well have been on Mars, rather than tucked in the South Dakota Badlands. Shane was still sweating from the fifteen-mile bike ride, which was nearly vertical in some places along the lonely trail and eventually led to an abandoned mine. They'd finally reached the spot known by the other endurance racers as Sheer Drop. It was a cliff of gray rock, striated with layers of black and white, studded with one lone tree standing sentinel against the sky. The view was spectacular. Even in his preoccupied state, Shane recognized the magnificence of the canyon below, twisting and brushy, and the hills with their covering of wind-tossed grass. The air was scented with the tang of newly fallen rain on long-parched ground.

Shane knew the Desert Quest race producers were keeping tabs on the participants. Back at the campground, which served as base of operations, they tracked everyone carefully via the GPS units all the racers carried, particularly Shane, as he was a late addition. He knew that race producer, Martin Chenko, and the man Shane was really interested in talking to, Devin Ackerman, were watching them.

Go ahead and watch, Ackerman. Enjoy things while you can.

A cold drizzle of rain snaked down his back as he laced

on his climbing shoes and secured the bike before beginning preparations for the descent, slipping on a harness and checking the static rope already affixed to the top of the cliff.

The bank of clouds blotted out the afternoon sky, and the wind blew in sporadic gusts. If the October drizzle morphed into a serious storm, the corrugated rocks would turn slick and rappelling down would be dangerous. Storms in the South Dakota Badlands were more than noisy. They were deadly. The man next to Shane regarded him without a hint of a smile, prematurely silver hair glinting in the sparse sunlight.

"Think you can make it? You've got to prove competency before they'll let us race as a team," Andy Gleeson said. "If you can't, say so now and I'll find another teammate. I'm in this thing to win the fifty thousand. My partner bugged out two weeks ago. That's the only reason I'm giving you a look."

"I got that. I can do it, if they don't call it on account of the weather. It's just a trial run."

"Seems to me you got a good incentive to win," Gleeson said, giving him an appraising look. "Ranching can't pay too good."

Shane started. "How did you know I'm a rancher?"

Gleeson looked at the sky. "Ah, you just hear things."

What things? Did Gleeson know about Shane's brother, even though he'd used a fake last name? If he did, then Ackerman might know the truth as well, the real reason Shane had entered the race. He itched to grill Gleeson, but further questions would only make things worse.

Shane jerked the strap on his helmet tight. "I know I'm your second choice." He also knew he could handle the physical requirements of the race. Climbing, swimming, canoeing and the like were no problem, after having spent plenty of time training for triathlons and Iron Man races.

The question was, could he accomplish his real goal? He knew deep down in his bones that race publicity man Devin Ackerman killed his sister-in-law, and all he had to do was find Ellen Brown, the woman who'd lied to give Ackerman an alibi. Many of the racers were repeaters so the chances were good some of Ellen's old teammates were competing again. All he needed was a way to contact her, convince her to come clean, at least enough to cast doubt on the police's ironclad case against his brother. Or maybe Ackerman would incriminate himself. Shane had done additional research, combing through blogs from previous Desert Quest races for any mention of Ackerman, and knew that the man liked to party. And when he did, he liked to talk.

All I need to do is stay around long enough to find the tiniest particle of truth, just enough to help Todd.

Gleeson checked the anchors. "Secure," he said.

Shane checked them again anyway, earning a nod of approval from his partner. A noise from down below drew his attention. A road followed the base of the cliff through pockets of smaller rock formations. A dark vehicle drove slowly along, heading in the direction of the campground. Shane watched the slow progress, wondering who would be driving up just then. Most of the racers were in camp, waiting out the storm, and the vehicle didn't have the Desert Quest markings on the side to identify it as a race official's.

He felt a spatter of rain on his face as the storm picked up, the wind tearing at his T-shirt. The car continued on, toward a small canyon, pinched in on both sides by rippled rock.

Gleeson rubbed his chin. "What do you think? Storm going to get worse?"

Shane didn't have to answer. A crackle of lightning sizzled overhead, followed a few moments later by the rumble of thunder that shook the sky and the ground under their feet. This high up, it seemed as though they were right in the center of the storm as the rain unleashed all its fury, howling around them.

They moved away from the tree toward a narrow outcropping of rock that would serve as scant shelter while Gleeson checked his satellite phone. "Message from HQ says we're officially postponing. We'll have to wait for a break and then take the bikes back." He looked up at the sky, face puckered in anger. "Why couldn't it have waited an hour? I wanted to get us qualified tonight."

Shane wasn't listening. From his position he could barely make out the car below as it entered the canyon. A memory of the past intruded, a time when his father had entered just such a canyon in just such a storm. One second it was clear, and the next they were nearly swallowed up by the crush of rising water.

Shane should have learned from that experience how deadly and unforgiving water could be.

If only he'd learned.

Somehow—with God's help, his brother had said—they'd escaped the flash flood then. He wondered if God was keeping tabs on that little car now.

Kelly Cloudman gripped the wheel as the wind shook the car. She glanced in the rearview at Charlie. Fortunately, the three-year-old was asleep, oblivious to her tension as they crept along. The walls of the canyon blotted out the meager light, leaving her straining to see. She sighed, wondering again why she was driving through the middle of nowhere, South Dakota, with Charlie.

Because he's yours now and he needs you.

She shot him another quick glance, noting the slight curl

in his hair and the round cheeks that matched those of her twin sister, Rose. They were fraternal twins, but Kelly and her sister had always been more alike than different—until her sister succumbed to alcoholism.

Where are you, Rose? What have you done?

She didn't know, in spite of her efforts and the half-hearted attempts by the police to locate Rose. Even their uncle Bill, who had returned to his job as Tribal Ranger after nearly losing his life and Heather's, the woman he would later marry, to a madman, had had no luck discovering the whereabouts of her vanished sister.

Sometimes she thought the whole thing was a dream. But the little child left in her car a year and a half ago was certainly not. Charlie was a flesh-and-blood child who desperately needed her. A vicious splatter of rain on the windshield made her jump.

"We'll be okay, Charlie," she whispered. "This job pays enough for us to find a place to stay until your mommy comes home." *If she ever does.* She swallowed the doubt.

Having a family hadn't been part of her vision. Not through college or the nursing school from which she'd just graduated a few months before. She'd been interested only in her academic pursuits—until a certain blue-eyed rancher had reminded her how incredibly joyful life could be.

Joyful…and devastating.

He's gone now, Kelly. He's got no place in your heart or your life anymore.

She'd gained a child and lost her soul mate, and now she was driving through a nasty storm to some desolate part of South Dakota she'd never laid eyes on before, even though she'd grown up in the state.

The rain fell harder now, slamming into the front windshield. She should have arrived for her job as race medic the day before, but Charlie had been sick and she was reluctant to make the drive when he was running a fever. Was this the way parenting was? The constant worry and rerouting of plans? She flashed on her own mother, who had struggled with drug addiction for years before she beat it. Sadly, her death had all the symptoms of an overdose, so Kelly and her sister had believed her to be a junkie right up to the very end. Guilt rose thick and cold inside her. She hadn't even been able to find Rose to tell her the truth—that their mother had been murdered. And she'd been so caught up in her own pursuits, she hadn't had much time for their mother until it was too late.

She pushed the hair out of her face. Motherhood was a complicated thing, an intricate connection between woman and child that persisted even when trauma and addiction got in the way. So far, hard as it had been to juggle her career and her role as a mom, she would not trade a minute of it. As if he heard her thoughts, Charlie started, suddenly awake.

"Mama Kelly," he said, brown eyes wide.

"It's okay, honey. I'm here." She had been floored when he decided to call her Mama, and somewhat awed by the responsibility of holding the title.

"Rain?"

"Yes, Charlie. It's raining. We'll be at the campground soon, okay?"

He pulled his flannel blanket with the trains printed on it to the side of his face and reached out to pet the elderly cat snuggled at his feet.

She looked again at the GPS fixed to the dashboard, which suddenly blinked to a blank screen.

"Don't quit on me now," she muttered, pushing down panic at the thought of being lost in this maze of twists and turns. At this point she just wanted to get out of the canyon. The sides were high, giving her the pinched, closed-in feeling that something bad was going to happen between those gray walls.

Stop being silly. You're driving through a storm, that's all.

Her stomach clenched into a tight ball as the storm let loose, pounding the roof of the car with fury.

Charlie whimpered, and the cat meowed her alarm.

"It's okay. We'll be fine in a minute. You just keep Paddy Paws company." The old cat settled down again, curled in a gray ball against Charlie's warm side, just like the day she found them both in the backseat of her car.

They were far from fine as the wheel failed to respond. Frantically she yanked it back and forth, to no avail, as the car drifted. The water began to fill the canyon, as if someone had turned on a giant faucet, causing the car to hydroplane. Willing herself not to scream, she wrenched ineffectively at the wheel. It began to turn in lazy circles until the car smacked into a rocky projection and lodged there. Flash flood, of course. She should have known it, shouldn't have made the stupid mistake of entering the canyon in these conditions.

She peered out the window, terrified to see the water rising steadily. It was cresting the bottom of the door and moving fast. If she didn't get Charlie out of that car, they would drown. The roar of the wind and rain was so loud she could not hear Charlie's crying now. She reached over the backseat and unbuckled him, pulling him to the front. He wrapped his arms and legs around her, burying his face in her neck, clutching his train blanket. Paddy leaped into the front seat, too.

With fingers gone cold, she unlocked the driver's door and pushed.

Nothing.

She kicked and slammed at it with all her might but the

door would not open, pushed tight by the force of the water outside, which now reached the bottom of the car window. Fighting down panic, she looked around for something to break the window. The jack was in the trunk.

Again she kicked at the door with every ounce of strength, but it would not open. Lightning scorched the sky, illuminating the terrifying flood outside the window. Thunder roared around them and they both cried out.

Heart in her throat, she watched the water rise, murmuring words of comfort that she did not believe to the terrified boy in her lap.

Shane continued to stare down into the howling storm that buffeted the little car below. He recognized the moment when the water overwhelmed the vehicle and it began to hydroplane. The car was now wedged against the rocks, and Shane had not seen anyone escape. Even if the driver had managed to shove open the door, he would have to be a strong swimmer to escape the flood that thundered past the car.

He didn't allow himself to think about it. Instead he trotted to the edge to hook up to the rappelling rope.

Gleeson yelled from behind. "What are you doing?"

"There's a car down there in trouble."

"You can't do that. They've closed the ropes course. Too dangerous."

Shane shot him a grin. "Do you know a faster way down?"

He watched Gleeson's openmouthed stare with a flicker of satisfaction as he slid over the side. The wind buffeted him back and forth as he rappelled down, his knees and elbows banging into the wet rocks on either side. He tried to keep the car in view during his descent, but the driving rain made it nearly impossible. At one point he began to twist helplessly, rocked by the violence of the storm, thunder splitting the air around him, until he regained some sense of balance and continued down dizzily to the bottom.

Unhooking quickly, he fought the disequilibrium and ran across the slippery ground in the direction of the car, thinking all the while that the driver could have used a dose of common sense. As little as two feet of water was enough to carry away a full-size car, and driving into a boxed-in canyon in the middle of a storm was a recipe for disaster.

Tripping on a root exposed by the torrential rain, he fell, skidding in the sandy earth for a yard or two before he regained his footing and pushed himself to go faster. The driver wouldn't have much time before the car was completely inundated. He reached the spot closest to the half-filled canyon where he could secure a rope to a sturdy pinnacle of rock. The wind tore at him as he lowered himself down. Water swirled up to the driver's window. Rain stung his eyes, and he could make out only the pale gleam of a face.

Pulling a flashlight from his belt, he yelled over the wind. "Get back!" It took two blows for the window to break. Hundreds of rounded bits of safety glass were snatched immediately away by the pull of the water now rushing in through the gap. Using his boot, he cleared as much of the remaining glass as he could and reached in to grab the person in the car. The tension in that slender arm was palpable as fingers locked around his. It took all Shane's strength to fight against the water, which poured into the car in a mighty tide.

Shoulders burning, he held tight to a handful of slippery fabric as he heaved with all his might until the figure pulled free and into his arms, clutching a wet bundle. He noted that it was a woman, long dark hair plastered over her face.

"We'll make for that ledge!" he yelled in her ear.

If she replied, he didn't hear as he fought against the water, which sucked at his waist and threatened to tear her out of his arms. Hand over hand, he pushed through the foam until they reached the relative safety of a small ledge, just above the water level.

He held on until the woman found a foothold and turned her face to his.

Something struck him as familiar about the dark eyes peeking from under the curtain of wet hair. Her hands were full of a bundle of some kind, and she jerked her head to clear the hair away.

His heart thumped to a stop.

Kelly.

He thought he'd gone mad.

"What?" he managed, so startled he almost lost his footing on the ledge.

Her eyes rounded as recognition dawned on her face. Her lips parted but she didn't speak.

"What are you doing here?" he finally managed.

Instead of answering, she pushed the bundle into his hands. The bundle turned out to be a little boy, face stark with terror.

And Kelly grabbed the trailing rope and plunged back toward the water.

TWO

Kelly didn't allow herself to acknowledge the shock of seeing Shane. She had another mission right now. The rope was wet and slick in her hands as she skidded down the rocks toward the rapidly filling car. She could faintly hear Charlie's high-pitched wail.

Don't worry, Charlie. I'll get her. I've got to get her.

The cat, that old bag of bones with the missing front tooth, was the only thing Charlie had left of his mother, and Kelly was not about to let the animal drown. Feet skidding, knees banging into the sharp rocks, she slid down the rope, grateful that she remembered a few things from her spelunking adventures with Shane in their happier days.

Shane was here. Right here, in this bit of South Dakota nowhere. Why?

She pushed away the thought. There was no time to indulge her feelings of betrayal now.

Find Paddy Paws.

Her feet hit the submerged trunk of the car. Water swirled around her ankles, so cold it took her breath away. She sloshed toward the broken driver's window, heart thudding, praying that the water hadn't overwhelmed the old cat and swept her away.

Gripping the edge of the window, she slid off the car and

into the water, which now poured around her torso. Pulling herself even with the window, she was elated to see Paddy Paws, wet and shivering, clinging to the headrest.

"Thank You, God," she whispered. "I'm here, Paddy. I'm coming to get you."

She reached out to the cat, and the terrified animal whisked up her arm, clinging to her back, claws sinking into her skin. Though the pain brought tears to her eyes, she persevered, finding the rope in the water and hauling herself onto the trunk in preparation to climb back up, when the car suddenly lurched. Jerked backward, Kelly toppled into the flood, fighting panic as the water closed over her head. Her eyes burned, and she tumbled so violently she could not decide which way led to the surface. Waves tugged and pulled at her, letting go long enough for her to suck in a breath, coughing and sputtering. In spite of her frantic splashing, she felt the press of water sucking her back under.

She tried to fight her way back to the rock wall, but the ferocious violence of the water sent her spiraling. Her lungs burned and pain shot through her as she banged into rocks that tumbled loose in the water.

Something grabbed her by the jacket and she fought to free herself.

She couldn't get loose. Eyes stinging and lungs burning, she broke the surface and found herself firmly in the grip of Shane Mason. His eyes glittered in a pale face, a sheaf of wet bangs plastered over his forehead, stubble of beard catching the droplets that ran down his face. He held a rope with one hand and quickly tied it around her waist.

"I've got to get the cat…" she gasped.

He didn't let her finish, but yelled for someone to hoist her up. Then he disappeared into the thundering water.

Kelly was frozen to the spot, unsure if Shane had lost his footing or dived into the water intentionally. The tug of the rope at her waist left her no time to ponder as she was slowly hauled up to the top. All the while her eyes pored over the flooded canyon for any sign of Shane or Paddy. Her heart squeezed. Had she just made him risk his life?

She gritted her teeth to stop them from chattering and peered into the water until she crested the top of the canyon. A big, crew-cut man with silver hair helped her over the edge. He looked familiar, though she couldn't place him.

Water beaded in the deep grooves on his forehead. "You all right?"

Her head spun, still dizzy from being tumbled like laundry in the wash. "Where's Charlie?"

"The boy's okay." He pointed to Charlie, who was now wrapped in a slicker and sitting in the front seat of a van, being tended to by a lady with a thick braid.

She felt a surge of relief as she followed the man back to the edge. They both peered down into the violent water.

"Do you see him?" she whispered, a ripple of dread surging through her.

"Not yet, but he's a strong swimmer. Must have slipped off the rocks when he was helping you."

She heard the condemnation in the man's voice. "What can we do?"

"Nothing," he said, his face grim. "It's up to him now."

The minutes ticked by in painful slow motion.

Slowly, the rain died away, leaving the canyon quiet except for the rush of water and the crackle of the radio as the man relayed the situation to someone on the other end. Kelly felt as if she was trapped in some sort of bad movie, only the script wasn't quite right. It was not her love who fought for his life below. Shane was a man she used to love, until he turned out to be someone else. Now he was just a stranger.

A stranger who had put his life at risk for hers.

Anger pricked her insides. Why had he bothered?

The answer came quickly. Because he hadn't known it was her and Charlie. As far as he knew, it was some hapless traveler, and he'd lent a hand because it was in his character to do so. She wondered if she would have the chance to thank him before they parted ways again. Permanently.

She peered harder into the gloom, hoping he would reappear at any moment. She looked for Paddy Paws as well, and thought about the little boy waiting in the van for his cat's safe return. How would she tell him that Paddy was gone? Just like Rose? And how would she feel if Shane didn't come back?

The man gave her a nervous look. "Maybe you should go wait in the van. You're shivering."

She hardly heard him. A movement caught her eye at the base of the cliff some twenty feet away. "I just saw…"

He saw it, too, and they both ran, slipping and stumbling until they reached the overhanging rock. The man let down a rope, securing the other end and using his body as an anchor to take some of the weight.

Soon the rope grew taut as the bedraggled figure on the other end began to climb slowly to the top. Kelly found the tension in her gut ratcheting up the closer he came until Shane appeared, face contorted with effort.

As the man heaved backward on the rope, Shane crawled over and made it to his feet. His face was torn and bleeding, but the eyes—those eyes which she knew to be a startling blue—were lively as ever. Her legs trembled.

There was nothing in his hands. Even Shane, the unstoppable outdoorsman, hadn't been able to save Paddy.

She swallowed hard, her nurse's training overriding the strange feeling of misery and relief that coursed through her. She ran to him, stopping so quickly her feet skidded on the slick ground. "Are you hurt?"

He shook the water from his hair. "Only scratched." She saw several sets of parallel gouges on his exposed forearms and one nasty set on his cheek.

Her eyes widened. "Did you…?"

He reached inside his shirt and pulled out a very wet and terrified cat. "So tell me why I nearly killed myself to save this ungrateful cat?"

Shane watched Kelly's face shift from unsettled to joyful in a quick second.

Her expression made his chest tighten.

"Paddy," she cried, scooping the soggy cat from his arms.

He watched her stroke the exhausted animal, grateful for the darkness that covered his rush of emotion. He'd grown used to surprises, even craved them, but this one left him reeling. Kelly Cloudman. Here. Her smile fired every nerve inside him.

He saw from the uncertainty on her face that she was as disarmed as he was.

"Thank you," she said finally. "For helping me and Paddy."

He shrugged. "I was in the neighborhood."

Gleeson broke in. "Matthews, you were supposed to be standing down until the storm passed. Didn't you hear me say Ackerman ordered us off?"

Shane slicked his wet hair out of his face and kept his eyes on Gleeson, praying Kelly would not ask about his fictional last name. "I don't take orders from Ackerman or anyone else."

Gleeson's chin went up. "Yeah? Well, you may have just cost yourself a spot in the race."

Shane shrugged. "So be it."

"So be it?" Gleeson seemed to puff up in anger. "Listen, kid. I gave you a shot and took you on as a partner, but you still have to meet the qualifications and you definitely have to follow orders. I'm in this thing to win, and I don't need you going cowboy and messing things up for me."

A woman Shane recognized as a fellow racer got out of the van and joined them in time to hear Gleeson's outburst. "He had a good reason."

Gleeson wasn't mollified. "He risked his life without a word. Didn't even radio for help. That's the kind of thing that will make Ackerman kick you out of the race, and I don't have time to keep finding new partners."

The woman held up a placating hand. "I'll talk to Devin. Explain things. He's quick-tempered but he's got a soft spot for women and cats." She cast a curious glance at Kelly. "Devin is my fiancé so I should know. I'm Betsy Falco. I'm competing in Desert Quest."

Kelly offered her free hand to Betsy and Gleeson. "I'm Kelly Cloudman, and this is Paddy Paws."

Betsy smiled. "Pleasure. I'm racing with my cousin, Gwen. She's back at camp because we already did the ropes prelim. I'm glad I decided to drive along and watch these guys, or I would have missed all the excitement. Are you a racer, Kelly? Can't think of any other reason you'd be out here, especially with your son."

Shane flushed. The effort of his clumsy water rescue had driven thoughts of the little boy out of his head. Now he glanced toward the van at the tiny bundled figure wrapped in the too-big slicker.

Kelly kept her eyes away from him as she answered. "He's my nephew. We were on our way to the campground. I'm the race medic."

Shane almost yelped. "What?"

Kelly finally looked at him, her face a mix of sadness and anger. "I needed a job," she said simply. "Charlie and I wanted to be closer to my uncle Bill anyway, and his wife, Heather, and my aunt Jean said she would help take care of him during the race events. She's joining me tomorrow. If I had known…"

If she had known he was a race participant, she never would have come. The words cut right through him. It couldn't be. He was here to catch a killer, and he didn't care what he had to risk to accomplish his task. But Kelly? He looked back to the van.

The boy's soft round cheeks and chubby hand pressed to the window brought back memories of his little brother, and the pain almost swept him away until Gleeson smacked him on the shoulder. "You okay? You look washed up."

He tried for a smile. "Rough swim."

Kelly nodded at them and returned to the van, her slender figure hunched against the violent wind. He heard a low squeal of joy as she handed the cat back to Charlie.

"You should get her back," Betsy said.

He started until he realized that she hadn't meant the words the way he heard them. "I'll stay with the bikes. You two drive the van to the campground and come back for me and the gear."

Gleeson looked at the sky. "Going to storm some more. Not much shelter here."

Not much shelter anywhere from the angry storm inside him. "Go on. Take care of her. I'll be here."

He watched them load up into the van, Gleeson at the wheel and Betsy next to him. Kelly sat in the back now, with Charlie, her long brown hair spiraling into endless curls from the soaking. The cuts the cat had given him burned now, though he felt nothing but cold, the deep-down cold that rooted inside him the moment he'd betrayed Kelly Cloudman.

* * *

Kelly found herself sitting in the backseat of the van, her arm around Charlie and Paddy Paws on her lap. Gleeson drove slowly, and Betsy turned often from her spot in the passenger seat to fill Kelly in on race preparations. The gist of it she already knew; it was broken into three tortuous legs: mountain biking, a canoe and run, and the spelunking/ropes course. Each racer was timed, and the team with the fastest cumulative time at the end of the three events would be the winner.

"The weather's been terrible so far. Of course, we're not scheduled to start for another day but there are a lot of racers who came early to pass their competency tests and get some extra practice in. The campground is nice and quiet, and the trailers are okay."

Kelly's mind wandered as Betsy chattered on. The past few hours felt like a dream, or maybe, more appropriately, a nightmare. Of all the people in the world to rescue her and Charlie at that moment, it had to be Shane. She wanted to forget him, to erase their time together. Absently, she rubbed her palms on her lap.

She blinked away the memories. The important thing was the little boy sitting next to her, humming to himself. Charlie was unharmed, and his precious feline companion had survived, too. She breathed a thank-you prayer.

Looking out into the black sky, too cloud-washed to reveal any stars, the detail returned that had been lurking just out of reach in her mind. Matthews. Gleeson had referred to Shane as Matthews, instead of Mason. He could have misspoken, but Shane's quick reaction, the barest flick of a glance in her direction, told Kelly it was not a mistake.

For some reason she could not fathom, Shane was using a fictitious last name. She wondered if it had something to do with the terrible news she'd heard the year before, the murder of Olivia Mason, Shane's sister-in-law.

I should have called. Should have written.

There were plenty of good reasons not to at the time. She was desperately trying to finish her nursing degree and dealing with an emotionally traumatized toddler, not to mention wrestling with her own anguish at Shane's abrupt departure from her life.

She still didn't understand what had happened to them. Maybe she never would, but she should have expressed her condolences when Olivia died. Shane loved Olivia like a sister and adored his brother, Todd. She should not have let her own anger and hurt keep her from doing the decent thing.

Forgive me, Lord.

Her clothes were clammy, clinging to her like a second soggy skin as the van pressed through the darkness for miles. Ahead she could just make out some lights as they drove into a flat basin, ringed by distant cliffs. It was hard to discern much, but as they passed through the split-rail fence she noticed a half-dozen small cottages, some dark and others with windows illuminated.

"Those are the cabins," Betsy said. "Mr. Chenko stays in one; he's the race producer. Devin's in another, and there are a few more race officials in the others. The rest of us lowly racers are in the trailers." She smiled. "Pretty luxurious for an endurance race, I think. Electricity, beds and all the good stuff."

"Have you done this kind of race before?"

"Nothing this big. I got interested after Devin and I met." She squinted to read the numbers on the electrical boxes outside the trailers. "Here you are, number seven. I'll go get the key in the office. Be right back."

Kelly shivered as they got out. She kept a firm arm around Paddy and held Charlie's hand tight.

"Mama Kelly?"

She smiled at him. "We're here, Charlie. This is where we're going to be staying."

He gave it a look and then pressed his tired face against her leg, heedless of the damp denim. She found Gleeson looking at them. With a start she placed his face. "I patched up your knee at the clinic."

"Yes, you did. Good as new." He eyed Charlie. "Nice little kid. Glad he's okay."

"Me, too."

"I have a son, but he's grown now."

"Does he live close by?"

"I wouldn't know. He doesn't speak to me, thanks to my ex." His eyes narrowed. "You know, for a minute, I got the sense that you and Matthews knew each other."

"Really?" Kelly's heart pounded. Should she reveal the truth? But there was some reason why Shane hadn't given this man his real name. She fussed with Charlie's hair, buying time, wondering what to say.

She was spared having to answer when Betsy arrived with another woman, much shorter than Betsy, with a mane of wild curly black hair. The woman cradled a bundle in her arms.

Betsy opened the door to the trailer as she talked. "This is my cousin, Gwen. She's petite, like you, so she has some dry clothes for you to wear and a T-shirt for Charlie to sleep in."

Kelly realized that all her possessions—everything from her phone to their pajamas—were underwater. She groaned.

"It's okay," Betsy said, reading her look. "We'll get the car towed out after the water drains away. You'd be surprised how fast that flood will be gone."

The interior of the trailer was worn, but clean. There was a full-size bed at one end and a set of little bunk beds at the other. A tiny kitchen tiled in yellowed linoleum and a minuscule bathroom rounded out the space. Kelly placed Paddy Paws on the floor, and she immediately scurried off to hide in the gap under the lowest bunk.

Betsy plopped a paper bag on the table. The trailer light picked up the glint in her copper hair.

"Some food in case you need a snack tonight. There's a small dining hall here that does breakfast." She grinned. "See? I told you this place was luxurious. I've got to go fill Devin in. I only radioed enough detail to let him know you all were okay. See you in the morning."

Gwen offered a shy smile and handed over the clothes. "Not much, but at least they're dry."

Kelly let out a heartfelt sigh. "Thank you. You have all been wonderful to us. We're so grateful." She picked Charlie up. "Let's say thank-you to Miss...?"

"Falco." Betsy had introduced Gwen as her cousin.

Charlie turned a sleepy face to Gwen and mumbled a thank-you.

Gwen took a step backward, her eyes glued on the boy, a stricken look on her face.

"Is everything okay?" Kelly asked, puzzled.

Her eyes remained riveted on Charlie. "He's so sweet. I'd love to have a son like that."

"He's my nephew, actually."

Gwen repeated the words as if they were some kind of chant. "Your nephew."

The silence became uncomfortable.

"Thank you again. I think I'd better get him into dry clothes."

Gwen seemed to snap out of her strange confusion. "Yes, right. I'll see you later then."

Kelly watched through the window as Gwen walked away from the trailer. Just before she left the circle of light from the porch lamp, she turned again, staring through the kitchen window, a disturbed look on her face.

Kelly felt a whisper of fear tickle her gut as she reached out and flicked the curtains closed.

THREE

Shane stood in the near darkness, watching the moonlight retreat and advance as clouds danced across the sky. He was cold and confused. Kelly could not be here. It was too much of a bizarre coincidence, and he did not believe in coincidences. She'd finished her nurses' training; he was not surprised about that. Kelly would do what she set out to, even if circumstances conspired against her. He'd always admired that about her.

The vibration of his satellite phone startled him. Heart hammering, he took it from its waterproof case and answered.

"Hey," his brother said, the jail phone connection crackling with static.

"Hey yourself. You sound funny." Shane tried to keep the worry out of his voice as he pictured his brother the last time he'd seen him—through the Plexiglas in the jail's visitors' room. The shock of seeing Todd in an orange jumpsuit still pained him.

"Got a fat lip."

"How?"

Todd sighed. "Couple guys found out I used to be a cop back in the day."

Shane's blood ran cold. Once a cop, always a cop in

the eyes of the inmates. Todd might as well have a target painted on his forehead in that South Dakota jail. He pressed the phone to his mouth. "Tell the warden. They've got to give you some protection."

"Trial's coming up, then it will all be over."

Shane cupped the phone against the wind, wishing he could reach through the connection. "You're not going to be convicted for something you didn't do."

His brother hesitated. "Maybe I did it."

"Don't say that. You didn't kill Olivia. You loved your wife."

Todd sighed again, his voice flat and listless. "Things were tough between Olivia and me before then. We had a fight. I...I was drinking. I passed out, but maybe before that..."

Shane forced out a calm breath. "You and I both know that it was someone else, one of the race producers you hosted last year, the night before she was murdered. The young one, Devin Ackerman, was fawning over Olivia, you told me."

"Yeah, and that set me off. Olivia said I was being a jealous fool." He laughed. "She always told it like it was."

The tiny spark in Todd's voice as he spoke gave Shane a moment of optimism. "I talked to a cop who used to work with you. He never bought Ackerman's alibi—that girl Ellen Brown, who said Ackerman was with her the night of the murder. He told me he thinks she might have been lying. I've been looking for her. I'm going to talk to her, convince her to tell the truth. It might not get you out, but it will be enough to cast some reasonable doubt."

"Have you found her yet?"

Shane wished desperately he had another answer. He'd spent a month trying to track her down, with no success. "Not yet, but they let me in the race. I'm here right now.

Plenty of the participants are repeaters from last year. One of them is likely to know where she went, have an email address, something. If nothing else, maybe I can get into the past race files and find her."

"Maybe she's telling the truth."

"Then why would she disappear? And how did Ackerman's business card wind up on Olivia's desk?"

"It's a long shot."

"It's the only shot I can think of. All I've got to do is poke a hole in his alibi. The police will have to take a closer look at Ackerman. I'm sure…"

Todd cut him off. "Police did their thing. They couldn't disprove Ackerman's alibi. No evidence pointing to anyone but me. Ranch hand heard us arguing. Gunshot residue on my fingers. Case closed."

He wanted to shout at his brother, shake some spirit back into him. "You've got to believe in your own innocence. I do. I've never stopped."

Shane pictured him now, green eyes so like Shane's other brother, Lonnie, the little boy who had died before he even got to taste what life had to offer.

"I did, too, at first, but I'm not so sure anymore. I blacked out, I was drunk and I have a temper. If I killed my wife, I deserve to be here," Todd said softly.

"Stop talking like that. You don't deserve to be in prison for a murder you didn't commit," Shane hissed. "Someone killed your wife, and we both know who that was. All we've got to do is come up with evidence that casts a reasonable doubt that you did it, give your lawyer something to work with."

Todd spoke slowly and deliberately. "Listen to me, Shane. I want you to leave that race and not come back. You've had enough pain already. Walk away from this mess. Find Kelly and start over with her."

Shane felt his face flush. He spent every waking moment missing Kelly, the feel of her silken hair on his face, the smile that lit up the inside of his heart like a beacon. "I'm not walking away." He swallowed hard. "You're the only brother I've got now."

"There's nothing left for me."

"Yes, there is. You always say God will…"

"That's what I used to think, that He answered prayers, interceded for people who loved Him," Todd said.

That's what Todd had tried to teach Shane when Lonnie died, and then when things fell apart with Kelly. "Don't give up your faith, Todd," he said, fighting to keep his voice level. He felt like a hypocrite telling his brother to hold onto God when Shane could not do the same, but he did not want to see that part of his brother die. Todd's faith might be the only thing that kept him alive until Shane could figure out how to free him.

Todd spoke with a tone completely devoid of hope. "It doesn't make sense to me anymore. I can't make myself believe it now."

Fear coiled through Shane's gut. What could he say to save his brother? "I will keep fighting until we find out who killed Olivia. We'll hire another lawyer if we need to."

"No. Let it go and walk away, just as I said." Todd sighed. "Goodbye, Shane," he said as he hung up.

Swallowing a surge of desperation, he walked to the edge of the canyon. The rain tapered off and the water had begun to recede, as if a drain had suddenly been uncapped. Water sucked away into the parched land around it and beyond, lowering visibly as he watched.

Soon Kelly's car was clear—still jammed against the rocks, but accessible. He retied a rope and eased himself down again. This time the driver's-side door opened easily.

Avoiding the bits of glass, he reached for the keys left in the ignition.

He imagined how panicked she must have been, knowing that she could drown at any moment, along with Charlie.

It was too painful to contemplate, and far too uncomfortable picturing what the little boy must have felt watching the water rise.

Had Lonnie felt that way? Had he known that the water would soon overwhelm him? Was his last feeling before he drowned an all-encompassing terror?

Black despair filled him. His brother's words floated into his mind.

Let go, Shane. Lonnie's with God. Let that be enough.

But Todd was letting his faith slip away under the weight of his unjust incarceration. How could he save the brother who had saved him so many times? Cold water seeped into his already sodden pants.

He noticed a sheaf of papers stuck under the visor, miraculously dry. Thinking they might be important to Kelly, he took them, noticing a card clipped to the top.

Devin Ackerman, Desert Quest Publicity Coordinator.

There was a phone number below, and a scrawled message: *Kelly, looking forward to having you aboard. D*

The papers crumpled as his grip tightened. Ackerman had hired Kelly? Why? She was a newly minted nurse. Surely there were many people far more qualified for the job than she. But Kelly, with her dark eyes and gentle smile, would have appealed to him for other reasons.

His stomach tightened and his breathing grew shallow.

Even though Ackerman was engaged, he knew the man was unable to resist a beautiful girl. What's more, he'd heard that the race coordinator was not above pursuing women, married or otherwise. If Ellen Brown hadn't given him an alibi for the night of Olivia's murder… He ground his teeth, stowed the papers inside his jacket and unhooked the car seat from the back. Then he took the keys from the ignition and made his way to the trunk. He unlocked it and retrieved a small duffel bag, swallowing against the lump in his throat.

It was the same bag she'd lugged along on their river rafting adventure. He jerked it free and grabbed a smaller blue backpack with a train emblazoned on the front. He closed the trunk again and made his way clumsily back to the top in time to see Gleeson pull up in the van.

"See you got your bags packed," Gleeson joked.

Shane didn't respond as he got in. They drove for several miles in silence.

"I guess we've got our new medic now," Gleeson said, giving him a quick glance.

"So it seems." Shane fumed. "How did Ackerman find Kelly?"

Gleeson tapped his fingers on the steering wheel. "Through me, actually. He met her when he took me to the clinic after I sprained my knee. She was real competent and looking for a job because her gig there was almost up." He grinned. "She's not bad to look at, either, so I think that already put her ahead of the previous medic."

Biting back a fiery remark, Shane forced himself to stare out the window. "What happened to the other medic?"

"Quit suddenly. Didn't give a reason that I'm aware of. Why you so interested?" Gleeson asked. "You know her?"

Shane wondered what Kelly had told him. Was Gleeson testing him?

He went for flippant. "I've met a lot of pretty girls. Who remembers?"

Gleeson chuckled.

Who remembers? Shane did—every moment of their time together was indelibly engraved on his mind. The smallest things remained there: the way her smile was higher on one side than the other, the curl of her hair right after she washed it, her laughter that always made him forget everything else. Her failed attempts at learning to cook, and all the truly awful food he'd eaten with a smile firmly plastered on his face.

"Anyway," Gleeson continued, "she's saddled with a kid. Don't know why anyone would sign on to hook up with that."

A kid. The comment circled in his mind, stabbing and biting like an angry beast. Is that what Kelly thought? That he'd left because he didn't want to be saddled with a kid? How could he ever tell her the truth?

He leaned his head back and let the miles go by, uncertain why the situation had taken such a strange turn. There was only one thing he knew for sure—Kelly had to leave. Immediately. The thought carried him back to the campground where he parted with Gleeson, shouldering the bags to take to Kelly's trailer, the one with the Team Medic placard displayed in the kitchen window.

The curtains were drawn and his hands felt clammy, heart hammering erratically.

Convince her to leave. That's all you have to do.

In an effort not to wake Charlie if the child was sleeping, Shane knocked softly.

Kelly answered, dressed in a pair of sweatpants that were too big and an oversized T-shirt. Her hair was still wet, but pulled up into a high ponytail. Even in clothes that didn't fit, after a harrowing near-death experience, she was still the most beautiful woman he'd ever seen, and for a moment he couldn't speak.

Kelly eyed the bags in his hands. "You didn't have to bring those."

Shane shrugged. "Concierge service included with your

luxury accommodations. Car will need to be towed, but I figured you might be able to use some of these things after they dry out." He hesitated. "Can I come in?"

She gave him a long look before she opened the door. "Just for a minute. Charlie is sleeping. I…we've been looking for his mother but no luck so he's got to settle for me. Guess I didn't do so well tonight."

He saw a little bundle in the full-size bed. "Is he okay?"

"Yes." She took a breath. "Thank you again. I'm not sure what would have happened if you hadn't come along."

He could see in her face the effort it took to say those words to him, the man she despised. "Forget it." He shot another glance at the boy, only the top of his head visible from under the blankets. He looked so small in the bed. "Any word on your sister?"

Kelly's face shimmered with pain. "My uncle has a lead, but so far nothing concrete."

"I hope she turns up safe."

"Me, too." She hugged herself. "I don't mean to be rude, but it's late. I've got to start work tomorrow so I think I'd better get some sleep."

"I need to talk to you about that."

Kelly cocked her head at him. "I think I know what you're going to say. I'm sorry that it's going to be a little awkward, Shane, but I had no idea you'd be here. We'll stay away from each other. One week and the whole thing will be over. You can stand it for that long, can't you?"

He winced. "That's not what I meant."

She frowned, the dim kitchen light reflecting in the dark pools of her eyes. "What, then? Does this have something to do with the fictitious name you're using?"

"Yes. Did you tell Gleeson we…know each other?"

"No. I'm not sure why, but I didn't. That was almost two years ago. Old history. What's going on?"

Their time together, though only a year, would never be old history in his mind. "I can't tell you."

"Why not?"

"Because it might put you in danger."

Anger flickered to life in her face. "You know, I've become pretty good at taking care of myself and Charlie."

He felt his cheeks flush, and he looked at his wet boots.

She waited a moment. "Fine, don't tell me, I'm not sure I want to know anyway. Say what you need to say. I've got to get some sleep."

He took a deep breath. "Kelly, you need to leave Desert Quest."

Kelly felt as if she must be dreaming. All the long evenings she'd sat in the secondhand rocking chair, comforting a wailing Charlie. Half the time during those endless nights, she found herself wishing Shane would walk back into her life, and the rest wishing she'd never met him in the first place. Now that he stood there, blond hair dark with moisture, full lips drawn tightly together and the fire in his blue eyes as strong as ever, her feelings flared into the same confused mess she'd experienced those earlier days. She was not sure whether to be furious or concerned.

"You can't just walk in here and tell me to leave my job. Working for Desert Quest is an incredible opportunity, and it's going to help me and Charlie buy a place closer to the city where I can find a job to support us both until my sister comes back."

He shifted. "I know it sounds crazy, but the people here are not who they seem to be."

"What do you mean?"

He walked to the window and opened one of the curtains to check out the other trailers. No one was watching, at least that he could see, and if anyone was, he was just returning

Kelly's belongings. "It would be better if you just trusted me and left."

She tried not to gape. "Trusted you? How can you even ask that after you walked out on me?" She fought for calm. "All your professed love evaporated as soon as you got wind of Charlie. The responsibility scared the love right out of you. That's a guy I'm supposed to trust again?"

"That isn't why…" He broke off. His voice was low and soft when he answered. "I guess not, but I'm asking you to anyway."

She bit down on her impatience. "Why? What's going on here? I'm not leaving, so you might as well tell me."

"Did Devin Ackerman hire you?"

She shrugged. "He told me his boss, Martin Chenko, did."

"On Ackerman's recommendation?"

"I suppose. Devin brought Gleeson into the clinic. I was just subbing there for a girl on maternity leave so it was actually my last week. He liked my work, and I suppose he recommended me to Mr. Chenko."

"Don't trust Ackerman, Kelly. You've got to get away from him."

"Why?" Her voice came out louder than she'd intended. Charlie stirred in the bed, and she lowered her volume. "What do you know about him?"

Shane turned determined eyes on her. "He killed Olivia."

"How…?" She tried again, head still whirling from the shock. "How do you know that?"

"There are lots of reasons which would take too long to give you now. Main point is my brother is in jail awaiting a murder trial for killing his wife, while Ackerman is the real killer."

"I'm sorry about Todd. I know how much you love him." The truth finally dawned on her. "So that's why you entered this race? To wander around pretending to be a racer to somehow find proof that Ackerman is guilty? That's not much of a plan."

"I'm going to find a lead to locate Ellen Brown, the woman who provided Ackerman's alibi. Someone here will know how to find her. Many of these people raced with her last year."

"Shane, that's crazy. You're desperate to help your brother—I get that—I feel the same way about my sister. But this isn't logical or rational."

"I'm past rational." Shane's faced blazed with emotion. "We mortgaged the ranch and hired the best lawyer we could afford, and you know what? It still looks like Todd is going to be convicted, even though I know he's innocent."

"Just because he's innocent doesn't make Ackerman guilty."

Shane shook his head. "I'm not going to get into the details. Please, Kelly. I want you to leave before you get hurt."

The look he gave her made her feel dizzy, as if she'd just stepped off a merry-go-round. That face that had lit up at the sight of her, the mouth that kissed her with the promise of forever, the mischievous eyes that looked at her now, shimmering with loss and heartbreak. Whether or not Shane was right about Ackerman, he believed wholeheartedly that the man was a killer.

She glanced over at Charlie. He was so small and vulnerable, and he had experienced more pain than a child ever should. She straightened. "I've already been hurt worse than I ever imagined, and I'm not leaving."

Shane was still, as if he was in another place with his thoughts. Then he nodded. "I'll let you get some sleep now."

She watched him walk into the darkness, headed for the trailer two spaces away from hers, head bowed against the heavy mist. He didn't look back at her, and she found her-self oddly disappointed.

Follow your own advice, Kelly. Stay away from him, and the whole thing will be over soon enough.

She saw him fish the key out of his pocket. Then he stiff-ened, head cocked.

Something about the posture made her hold her breath. The weak porch light cast shadows against the trailer as he stood there, key in hand. She watched as he backed quietly away, before she poked her head out of her trailer door.

"What is it, Shane?" she whispered.

He darted a look at her.

"Someone's in my trailer. Go inside and lock your door."

Her body grew cold. "What are you going to do?"

He flashed her an almost grin, reminding her of the cocky Shane Mason she used to know. And love.

Then he vanished into the shadows. Kelly followed his advice and shut herself inside, but she opened the curtains and slid the window open. Heart in her throat, she consid-ered calling someone to help Shane, until she remembered that her phone was on the floor of her car, wedged in the canyon. There was no one to call anyway, except Uncle Bill—and he was nearly two hours away.

The air was heavy with the promise of more rain. Drop-lets of mist danced in the air near the various porch lights, leaving the rest of the area cloaked in darkness, redolent with the scent of wet earth. She strained to make out any sign of Shane. It was quiet, except for the clunk of wet pine needles falling now and again to the metal roof of the trailer.

The situation was nearly preposterous as she considered Shane's wild allegations against Ackerman and his plan to pose as a racer to sniff out proof. She knew he was grief-stricken, so consumed by worry for his brother that he'd convinced himself Devin was some sort of calculating murderer. Her heart squeezed at the thought of his paranoia. He was not like the Shane she'd known, brash and unafraid of anything.

Except when Charlie had showed up.

Through all the anger and hurt at his abandonment, she could not shake the notion that there was a strange and unaccountable fear inside him. She'd just turned to check on Charlie when a shout cut through the silence. Out in the darkness, she saw a blur of movement. Shane? Someone else? She couldn't tell.

Another shout brought her out on the front porch and into the night. She ran toward the sound until Shane barreled around the corner. "What happened?"

He was breathing hard and unable to answer when Devin Ackerman jogged up. "What's going on?" he demanded, hands on his hips. His dark hair was expensively cut, a tiny diamond stud winking in his ear.

Shane straightened. "Someone was in my trailer, going through my stuff."

Devin blinked. "Who would want to do that?"

They were interrupted by the arrival of Martin Chenko on a golf cart. He pulled to a stop in time to hear Shane's explanation. He stepped out of the golf cart and smiled broadly, his stocky frame a few inches shorter than Devin's. Kelly guessed him to be in his early forties, fit and hearty. "What's going on?" he asked.

Devin explained. "I'm sure it was nothing. Probably someone got disoriented and went into your trailer by mistake."

Shane fixed Chenko with a dubious look. "The lock was picked. I thought I saw someone running away."

Chenko's thick eyebrows shot up. "Now why would anyone want to do that?"

Devin laughed. "When I heard you shouting, I thought

someone had set their trailer on fire." He clapped Shane on the shoulder. "It's your imagination. You probably left your door unlocked. Too much late-night TV."

Kelly saw Shane stiffen, but he did not pull away.

"We don't have any dishonest racers around here, now do we?" Devin asked.

Kelly thought there was a challenge in Devin's eyes before he turned to her.

"Kelly," he said, clasping her hands in his, long fingers wrapping around hers. "I'm so glad you're okay after what you've been through today. It's like a bad movie or something."

She wanted to pull away, disentangle herself from his grasp. "It turned out okay, thanks to Shane."

Devin didn't look at him. "I'm relieved."

She finally managed to pull her fingers from his when Chenko spoke. "Wouldn't do to lose our nurse before we even kicked off the race. So glad you're okay. And the boy, too? Charlie? Is he all right?"

"Perfectly fine, thank the Lord."

"How did you make it here so fast?" Shane asked Devin.

"I was out for a walk."

Shane stared at him. "Bad weather for a stroll."

A flicker of emotion passed across Devin's face, but the smile never faded. "I'm not afraid of a little water. Lucky you aren't, either. Lucky for Kelly here, too. We watched your progress via your GPS, but by the time we got close enough to help, you'd done your hero thing."

Shane shrugged.

Chenko sighed. "It's chilly out here. How about we all go to my cottage and we'll have some coffee? I was just looking over the routes again and trying to think of some alternate plans if the rain continues."

Shane shook his head. "No, thanks."

Devin turned to Kelly. "We really just want to meet this lovely lady anyway," he said with a chuckle. "How about it, Ms. Cloudman? Coffee? It's boring just talking to Chenko, no offense."

Chenko shook his head in amusement. "I'm a business-man, not an entertainer."

Kelly felt Shane's gaze boring into her, though she didn't meet his eyes. "Thanks very much, but I need to get back to Charlie."

She walked to her trailer, suddenly feeling a strange anxiety building in her stomach. Increasing her pace, she covered the ground quickly, confusion roiling through her. Shane's wild accusations, Devin's overly friendly gestures and her near drowning crowded through her mind, and she felt desperate to cocoon herself in her trailer with Charlie cradled in her arms. Entering quietly, she heaved a sigh of relief.

The horrible night was over. At least she could hold on to that. She breathed a prayer of thanks and eased off the flip-flops Gwen had loaned her, tiptoeing into the tiny bed-room.

Her heart thunked to a painful stop when reality hit home.

Charlie was gone.

FOUR

Kelly could not make a sound. Terror pricked her skin and froze her vocal cords. She ran to the bed and flung the covers off, checking underneath and in the small closets.

No Charlie.

She slammed into the small bathroom and checked every cupboard and cranny.

He was gone. Charlie was gone.

Body moving in spite of her fear, she ran out the front of the trailer, the door banging into the metal siding. Chenko and Devin were in the golf cart, headed back toward their cabins.

"Help!" she screamed, but they were too far away. She whirled in a circle, looking for some sign of the little boy. A light rain fell in icy needles, but she did not feel it.

"Charlie!" she yelled over the pattering drizzle.

Then Shane was there, turning her in his arms. "What is it?"

"Charlie's gone. He's not in the trailer." She looked helplessly around until her eyes went toward the riverbed beyond the campground.

A strange look crossed Shane's face as he followed her gaze, a mix of disbelief and horror. Without a word, he turned and ran toward the water. She was about to follow, when a flicker of movement caught her eye. Several yards away, illuminated by a porch light fixed to the side of the lodge, she saw a woman holding something.

Kelly moved closer until she could make out that the bundle in the woman's arms was a boy.

Charlie.

She ran, yelling his name, and the woman looked up. It was Gwen, her face eerie in the dim light, a faraway look on her face amid the swirl of hair.

"Charlie," Kelly said, tears on her face. Gwen held him out and she pulled him into her arms. "What happened?"

Gwen blinked. "He was walking around looking for you. I was going to bring him back to your trailer."

"Walking around?" She looked at Charlie, who seemed dazed. He had been known to sleepwalk when he was disturbed about something, and the day had been traumatic, to say the least. Had he awakened and been disoriented? She kissed his forehead and tucked him under her chin, gently squeezing the comforting weight of him to reassure herself that he was really there, safe, unhurt.

Forcing in a calming breath, she looked at Gwen. "Thank you for finding him."

Gwen's eyes were fixed on Charlie. "He's so sweet."

"Yes, he is."

Droplets of water collected on her hair. "You're lucky to have him."

Something in the way she said it, the longing in her voice, made Kelly draw back a pace. "Definitely. Thank you again, Gwen."

She nodded and shoved her hands in her pockets before she walked into the rain.

Kelly hunched her shoulders to keep the cold wind off Charlie as she headed back to the trailer. Shane ran up, face wild and desperate until he saw her holding the boy. The emotion shimmered on his face, intensified perhaps by the watery moonlight, and it confused Kelly. The raw anguish she saw there disappeared under an easy smile.

"He's okay, Kell?"

"Gwen found him sleepwalking."

Shane opened the door for her as she eased Charlie up the steps. She unwrapped him from the wet blanket, and he blinked at her.

"Charlie, honey, did you go outside?"

He mumbled something and allowed Kelly to ease him under the covers.

Shane gave her a questioning look as they tiptoed into the kitchen area.

"He sleepwalks sometimes when he's upset."

Shane nodded. "The flood?"

"Probably."

He cocked his head, water droplets plunking softly to the floor. "Why do you look worried?"

She stiffened and turned away to drape the blanket over a chair. "It's nothing."

He put his hand out and gently caressed her shoulder. "Nope. I can tell when nothing is something. You used to call me a mind reader, remember?"

She felt the flicker of familiar comfort from his touch, hands that had held and reassured her, thrilled and strengthened her. Pulling away, she turned to face him. "Maybe you can't read me so well anymore, Shane."

"And maybe I can." He fixed her with eyes so intense, she could not look away. "You think something isn't right."

She folded her arms. "Not really. It's just that Gwen is…" She struggled to find the words.

"Hiding something? I'm not surprised. Gwen turns up with Charlie, and Gleeson seems to know more about me than he should. Good reasons to pack up and go."

"But you're staying."

"I have to. My brother is out of options." He reached out to her, but she did not let him touch her.

"Go, Kelly. Take off while you can."

"I'm not going."

He sighed, a defeated look coming over his face. "We'll leave it for now. We can talk more in the morning. Lock up, okay?"

She turned the bolt as soon as Shane left, stifling her instinct to peek out the window and watch him leave. Slipping off her damp clothes and pulling on an oversized T-shirt, she crawled under the covers next to Charlie and listened to the reassuring ebb and flow of his breathing. Paddy Paws joined them.

Kelly whispered a prayer of profound gratitude and turned off the light. Closing her eyes, she remembered Shane's expression as he came up from the river. She had never seen Shane Mason afraid of anything, but the anguish written on his face spoke of something from the past, something dark and terrifying imprinted on his soul.

Shivering, she pulled the blankets tighter and fell into an uneasy sleep.

Shane awoke to Gleeson pounding on his door the next morning. His body complained from the rough treatment the previous night as he greeted Gleeson.

"Good news," Gleeson bellowed as he clapped Shane on the shoulder. "After your idiot stunt on the ropes yesterday, Chenko approved you to race. We're good to go for a one o'clock prelim to familiarize everyone with the course. Then we start tomorrow."

Shane blinked. "One o'clock. Got it."

Gleeson looked around the trailer. "Heard you thought someone broke in."

"How'd you hear that?"

"Ackerman told me this morning. Said you're crazy to think someone here would rifle through your stuff."

"That's me. Crazy Shane."

Gleeson's smile vanished. "Not making too many friends, Matthews. Folks don't like being accused."

"I haven't accused anyone. Yet."

Gleeson's eyes narrowed. After a moment he smiled. "Whatever. All I care about is the prelim at 1:00. Have your bike ready, and we'll hope this rain doesn't delay things."

"Where's Ackerman?"

Gleeson looked surprised. "In the lodge eating breakfast, along with everyone else. Why?"

"Just wanted to check in on a few things."

"What things?"

Shane gave him a grin. "Nothing that concerns you, Mother Gleeson."

"Why did I ever take you on as a partner? You're gonna make trouble before this thing is over."

You have no idea. Shane followed him out. The morning was cool, water still dripping from the juniper trees that clustered around the campground. The sun had not yet fully risen, the weak light illuminating veils of clouds.

The lodge was crowded with racers clutching coffee cups and crowded around long tables. A breakfast of fruit, granola, scrambled eggs and juices was set up buffet-style in the corner. He scanned the room immediately for Kelly and Charlie, but he didn't spot them. Shane noticed Ackerman talking to Betsy, who laughed and toyed with her braid. Ackerman was sandwiched between chatting racers, and Shane couldn't get close so he poured himself some coffee and took a spot near the door. Chenko appeared at his elbow, looking tired. He lifted his cup in salute.

"Thank goodness for coffee," he said.

Shane nodded, taking in the shadows under the race producer's eyes. "Bad night?"

Chenko sighed. "It's the weather. You can circumvent nearly any race obstacle that arises, but not the weather. That annoys me."

"Have you cancelled races before?"

"Almost. Last year the weather was unpredictable, too. There was an accident on the riding leg of the race. Had to borrow horses from a local."

Shane stiffened. The locals, he knew, were his brother, Todd, and Olivia. A shadow crossed Chenko's face. "Nice folks helped us out. I was really sorry the gal was killed." Chenko shook his head. "You'd think that kinda thing wouldn't happen out here in God's country."

Shane imagined what his brother would say. It's all God's country, but anywhere there are people, bad things can happen. He wondered how his brother was doing, locked in a cage, the threads of his faith loosening like a flag fraying in a vicious wind. "Did you have the same team working for you then?"

Chenko raised an eyebrow. "Team?" He laughed. "By team, I suppose you mean Devin. Yeah, been with me for a couple years now. He's great with people, but he could use some schooling in business. It's all about connections and keeping your eye on the goal. He's got his sights on something else most of the time. As my daddy used to tell me, if you don't keep your eyes on the prize, someone else will take it." Chenko noticed a newcomer to the group, a mustached man with a bald head toting some serious camera power. "Speaking of which, if you'll excuse me, I smell publicity in the air."

Kelly arrived with a bright-eyed Charlie in her arms. Shane opened his mouth to call to her but closed it abruptly when Devin gestured her over. He whispered something to Betsy, who frowned for a moment before leaving the table.

Kelly sat next to Devin with Charlie on her lap. She looked rested, in spite of the harrowing night, slim and strong in the pair of jeans she must have popped in the camp dryer and a race T-shirt. He watched the three of them chatting, laughing, and his heart sank. Man, woman and child. A family. Though Kelly had echoed his desire to not have children, she seemed to have fallen into the mother role so naturally, so willingly.

And Charlie, the little boy with the wide brown eyes, put his hand up and rested it on her cheek.

The gesture knifed through him. Charlie needed Kelly, depended completely on her protection and care. Relied on her to keep him safe.

The terror he'd felt when he'd run down to the river flooded back into his gut.

Please...please don't let me see him there, face down in that water. Please...

He'd offered the plea automatically, like an ignorant child.

No one up there, Shane. No one for you.

He downed another slug of coffee, relieved when Kelly led Charlie away to prepare plates of food. Devin rose and hopped onto the tiny platform at one end of the lodge, tapping a cordless microphone.

"Good morning, racers. Today is your last day to back out before the official torture begins in the morning."

The racers responded with laughter and good-natured heckling. Devin turned on a small laptop computer and pulled down a screen. "The race is divided into three legs." He grinned. "You cowboy types were no doubt disappointed that we've eliminated the horseback part of the trip."

Shane stiffened, fighting the urge to stand up and ask

Devin to explain in front of everyone about the mishap and the ensuing visit to his brother's ranch the year before. He stayed put, though, and Devin's presentation flowed smoothly on, covering the particulars of the equipment and route. Someone settled into a chair next to him, and he was surprised to find Kelly and Charlie there.

Kelly's cheeks pinked. "Sorry. This was the only spot with two chairs, and Charlie does better when he's not sitting on my lap for breakfast."

Shane managed a smile. "Sure."

Kelly brushed some hair out of Charlie's face. "Charlie, this is Mr....Shane. He's a..." She flicked a quick look at him and then back to Charlie. "He's a racer, like the others."

And that's all he was to her. Just like the others. Like the mom who let her down and the other nameless faces that went in and out of her life. He forced a cheerful tone. "Hello, Charlie. Good to meet you. Do you like to ride bikes?"

Charlie nodded. "I gotta trike for Christmas."

"That's great." He watched Charlie tuck into his scrambled eggs, the fork seeming too large in his small fingers.

Kelly eyed Shane over the top of her coffee cup. She lowered her voice to a near whisper. "Shane..." Her words trailed off for a moment. "I was thinking about the reason you came here. It seems like a long shot to find a way to crack Ackerman's alibi."

Shane winced, wishing he hadn't been forced to tell her about the plan. "It's the only thing I can do to help my brother."

"My uncle Bill is back with the Tribal Rangers. Maybe he can help you."

Shane shook his head, surprised at the offer and fairly certain he would not get much help at all from Kelly's uncle after what had happened between him and Kelly. "I appreciate that," he said, looking around to be sure no one had overheard. The group was hanging on Ackerman's every word. "There's nothing he can do that the cops haven't already done."

"Don't be too sure. He's very persistent."

He couldn't hold back a smile. "Really?"

She returned the smile for a moment before the humor was replaced by a cool expression. "Anyway, it was just a thought. But you're not giving up—I can tell."

"Must be a family trait."

"I wouldn't have thought so."

The words stung. He looked away. She busied herself wiping Charlie's hands and face, looking around, he imagined, to find another spot to sit. She'd just finished her cleanup when Ackerman announced from the microphone, "Let's introduce you to our new race medic, Kelly Cloudman. Come on up here, Kelly."

Kelly flushed and walked to the platform. Charlie watched her. "That's my mama. I've got two. Mama Rose is on a trip."

Shane found himself unable to answer.

Charlie waved and knocked over his orange juice in the process. Instinctively, Shane threw the nearby napkins down on the spill and said in his best John Wayne voice, "No worries, Cowboy Charlie. We got the flood under control, partner."

Charlie laughed. "You're funny."

Funny. A memory of his little brother's laughter rolled through him.

Funny Shane. The goofy big brother who could always get a laugh.

Lonnie, whose laughter was swallowed up by Shane's carelessness in a moment that would change everything.

One horrible moment.

His reverie was broken at the sound of applause for Kelly. She waved, and Ackerman hugged her around the shoulder. Just a friendly gesture, a warm greeting that nonetheless made Shane want to launch himself at the platform and knock Ackerman away from her.

He gritted his teeth as Kelly detached herself and made her way back to the table, cheeks flushed.

"Embarrassing," she said.

Shane couldn't stop himself. "Stay away from him, Kell. He's not what he seems."

Her eyes flashed. "Ironic, coming from you." She helped Charlie from the chair and made her way to the back, holding him in her arms as Ackerman started up a computer presentation.

Shane felt like breaking something. She was stubborn and she would not listen to reason, especially when it came from him.

Do what you need to do to find Ellen.

He watched the handsome man, so at ease in front of the crowd. Hard to believe he could be a murderer. What if Kelly was right and he wasn't? The whole thing was some desperate effort that made no sense.

His hands balled into fists. No. Todd was right about people, and he'd pegged Devin as trouble. Todd's cop friend felt the same way. Pictures began to scroll across the screen of prior Desert Quest races. The first had been in Utah, the last two in South Dakota. Smiling, dirt-covered racers, engaged in everything from biking to kayaking to spelunking, waved back from the screen to the hoots and hollers of the audience. He saw a quick shot of Gleeson on horseback, which surprised him. The man had said nothing about participating in other Quest races.

The music swelled and filled the small trailer, the excitement palpable. Another picture materialized.

Shane's heart hammered to a stop.

It was a picture of Olivia, arm in arm with Betsy, smiling for the camera as vibrant and full of life as he remembered her. Just behind them was a slender blonde whom Shane knew was Ellen Brown from the news coverage of the murder.

Shane stiffened, locking eyes with Ackerman, whose smile faded. The picture quickly dissolved into the next one, and Ackerman's face was once again a portrait of charm.

Shane looked across the room at Kelly, who was staring at him. She'd seen Olivia's picture, too.

Had she seen Ackerman's reaction to the photo?

Kelly answered the question by turning away, swinging Charlie into her arms and applauding with the rest as the slide show ended.

FIVE

Kelly took Charlie outside and watched him play in the watery sunshine, collecting pine needles and small bits of rock. She could not get the picture of Olivia out of her mind. She'd never met her, but it was impossible to believe the smiling, vibrant woman from the photo had been murdered, especially by Devin Ackerman. She'd seen Devin's expression when the photo was shown, the flicker of unease, but it was likely because he had inadvertently left her picture in the slide show, a tasteless error in view of what had happened a few days before the race last year had commenced.

She'd seen the shock in Shane's face too, the grief etched there before anger took its place. When had he become so suspicious, so seized by the certainty of Ackerman's guilt? In the long months they had been apart, where had the happy, fun-loving Shane Mason gone? She remembered the haggard face that greeted her in the mirror that morning. Shane wasn't the only one who had changed in their time apart. Where had her enthusiasm gone?

Her thoughts were interrupted as a rickety pickup truck wheezed into camp. Kelly's spirit lifted as the sturdy grayhaired lady hopped out. Her wrinkled face was tanned and beaming.

"Aunt Jean," Kelly called, wrapping her arms around

the woman who seemed much younger than her sixty-eight years.

Aunt Jean squeezed her and planted a kiss on each of her cheeks. "Hello, sweetie. You look as pretty as a sunrise."

Kelly smiled, feeling herself relax for the first time in days. "I am so glad to see you."

"Glad you asked me to come. Delighted to be invited to take care of that precious boy. I've been counting the moments. Now where is my angel?"

Kelly called Charlie over. He smiled shyly and hid behind her leg. "You remember Aunt Jean, don't you, Charlie? We saw her…" Kelly trailed off. The last time Charlie had visited Aunt Jean was on his third birthday, the day that Rose had promised to visit.

The day she hadn't come. Another in a string of disappointments.

Now it was only a few days until Charlie's fourth birthday, and Kelly was desperate for the phone to ring, to know that her sister would come and see Charlie before he could no longer remember her at all. Kelly hadn't told Charlie his mother was going to visit. She could not stand to see the disappointment in his eyes again.

With a start, Kelly remembered that her phone had been destroyed. Had her sister tried to call? Kelly suppressed a groan.

"What's the matter?" Jean said, wiggling her fingers at Charlie.

"Nothing. We had a little accident on the way up and I lost my phone. I'll have to get a new one."

Charlie edged over to Jean, and the two solemnly shook hands before Jean swept him up and swung him around. His squeals of delight danced through the air, and Kelly momentarily forgot her troubles.

Charlie has a family. Maybe it didn't look quite the same

as other families, but she had done her best to make sure he felt loved and cherished, in spite of his absent mother. *We're a family,* she repeated to herself fiercely, *just me and Charlie, Aunt Jean, and Uncle Bill and Heather.*

And hopefully Rose.

She heard the racers start to stream out of the lodge. Shane would be among them, the man she had thought would become family and stand by her always, through anything.

How wrong she'd been. How utterly wrong.

Jean fished out a plastic car from her pocket and gave it to Charlie. "It's from your uncle Bill."

Charlie's face lit, and he scampered away to roll it along the bench of a nearby picnic table.

Jean squeezed Kelly around the shoulders. "So tell me about this accident. Your uncle will grill me when I get back, you know."

"Oh, everything's okay. I'm so glad you're here for Charlie. Monday's his birthday."

A shadow passed over Jean's face. "Yes. I brought some special things so we can have a little party. Bill will come if things are okay at home."

Kelly's uncle Bill and his new wife, Heather, were foster parents to young Tina Moon until her guardian recovered from a stroke. Tina had been a handful for the two of them. "I'd love to see them." She lowered her voice. "I haven't told Charlie that Rose is supposed to come."

Jean nodded. "I think that's wise."

Kelly caught Jean's frown as she watched Charlie play. "What's wrong, Aunt Jean?"

She opened her mouth to answer when Martin Chenko approached. "Hello, ma'am. You must be Miss Cloudman's aunt."

She shook his hand. "Call me Jean. Everyone does."

"Pleasure to meet you." He turned to Kelly. "Don't want to interrupt, but I heard your phone was swamped." He handed over a satellite phone. "Here's one you can use until the race is over."

Kelly thanked him profusely.

"It's nothing at all. I'll need to keep in touch throughout the race, and your family will want to talk to you, I'm sure."

Kelly gripped the phone. "I'm hoping to hear from my sister."

Chenko must have caught the urgent tone in her voice. "Problem?"

"No. It's Charlie's birthday on Monday, and she'll want to talk to him."

The strange expression crossed Aunt Jean's face again, and Kelly thought she might cry. Chenko must have noticed it, too. "Are you feeling well, ma'am?"

"Fine, fine," she said, walking over to Charlie.

Kelly frowned. Chenko gave her a puzzled look. "Did I say something wrong?"

"No, no. Thank you very much for the phone."

"No problem." He watched Charlie for a minute. "He likes cars, I see."

"Yes, he went through a train phase, but now it's nothing but cars."

Chenko laughed. "A boy after my own heart. When I was a boy, I had a Mustang that made me feel like the biggest man in the Dakotas."

"Do you have children?"

"No." He chuckled. "Not sure I'd be much good at it, even if I got the chance. Maybe I'll give it a try someday."

He was about to leave when an impulse struck her. "Mr. Chenko, are a lot of the racers repeaters from last year?"

"A couple dozen, I'd say. Some people are just addicted. Good thing for me."

"Like Betsy?"

He blinked. "This is her first race, but she hung around last year."

"Oh, that's why I saw Betsy's picture in the slide show from last year. And another woman, a young blonde."

He considered. "Can't remember who the blonde was. Betsy was involved in helping unofficially on the last Quest because she and Devin had started dating. She didn't want to let him out of her sight, I guess, so she was around all the time." He sighed. "Good thing she was helpful and didn't ask to be paid. That's my favorite kind of volunteer." He ambled away.

Kelly joined her family and escorted Aunt Jean to the trailer so she could get settled in. "Do you want to lie down for a while? We have to leave for the race site at noon, so you'll be on kid duty then."

"I've never napped in my life. I want Charlie to show me the campground. I saw a little play area as I came in, didn't I?"

Charlie did not need any further urging as he dragged a laughing Aunt Jean away. Quickly she sent a text to her sister: Here's my new phone number. Starting a different job and want to tell you about it. Where are you? Getting worried. K

Kelly locked the door of the trailer and headed to the playground, wondering when she would be able to find out the real reason for the worry on her aunt's face.

Shane found himself loading the bikes after checking them carefully. Perfect condition. He wished he could say as much for himself. Since he'd seen the slide of Olivia and Betsy, he couldn't get the unsettled feeling out of his gut. Added to that was the sight of Ackerman schmoozing the crowd, and Kelly, too. The guy was a menace.

"Easy there," Gleeson said as Shane yanked on the ropes, securing the bikes to the truck bed. "What's eating you?"

"Nothing."

Gleeson slid behind the wheel, and Shane took in the passenger seat. They fell in line in the caravan of racers, right behind the SUV with MEDIC lettered on the side, and in front of Gwen and Betsy's dented pickup. Kelly nodded to them as she passed, carrying her backpack filled with medical supplies, and got into her own vehicle. Shane felt his nerves tingle as they always did when he caught the swish of her dark hair, the hint of that impish smile. When would that longing go away?

Ackerman strode along easily, cameras and lenses dangling from his neck. He waved a hand at them before stopping at Kelly's car.

"Can you give me a lift? I've got so much gear I can't fit it all in Chenko's car."

Shane did not catch Kelly's reply, but Ackerman nodded and got in next to her.

The guy was a murderer, and Kelly was giving him a ride. Shane realized that he was grinding his teeth. He snuck a glance at Gleeson, who didn't seem to notice. "What do you know about Ackerman?"

Gleeson looked surprised. "Devin? Nice guy. Good with the girls. Probably because he's the only son, with three older sisters. Parents are highbrow, plenty of dough. Don't get the sense they'd be too happy about him slumming with a bunch of endurance racers. Why?"

"No reason."

Finally, the cars began to roll out toward the racecourse. He tried to enjoy the scenery as they went. The first leg of the race was a looping trail in mountainous country with long draws, high ridges and spectacular overlooks.

Though it was not his primary purpose in being there,

Shane still felt the competitive juices rising up. He loved pitting his body against the elements and emerging victorious. It gave him the fleeting sense that he was in control of his life, and nothing else mattered. Not relationships he'd ruined, or lives he'd lost.

The way grew bumpy as they neared the course, rising to follow a limestone rim through stands of pine and spruce. The October rains had awakened pockets of grass and clusters of Jimsonweed, their white flowers still twisted shut. Shane rolled down the window to suck in a lungful of air, so clean it cut right through him. He remembered riding trails like these with Kelly. With deli sandwiches and cold water in their packs and the open trail in front of them, he'd thought he had finally found the place he belonged, a place where the past and present did not collide.

But in spite of Shane's efforts, the past had a monstrous way of insinuating itself into his happiness. He shot a glance at Kelly as they pulled the cars to a stop and got out. She'd caught her fantastic mane of hair into a ponytail and put on a Desert Quest Medic baseball cap. Her face told him she was in nurse mode. No nonsense allowed.

Good, he thought, as he rolled their bikes to the top of the course. She'd have no patience for Devin's hollow charm. Leaving the bikes, they all flocked to the edge where they could get a glimpse of what lay in store. After fifteen minutes of conversation or so, Chenko joined them, clipboard in one hand and radio in the other. He went ahead a few yards down the trail, where there was a sharp drop-off on one side. He looked the trail over closely. Devin busied himself snapping pictures of the fifty racers who talked excitedly, pointing to various elements of the course.

Shane understood their excitement. The course offered a variety of trail conditions, from single to double track, packed dirt, grass and rock, steep climbs and heart-stopping descents. Every adrenaline junkie's dream. His muscles tensed with anticipation.

Chenko returned and gave them the thumbs-up. "It's wet, but not too bad. It will give all you racing nuts an extra thrill!"

There was a collective cheer and hooting from the group.

"Remember now," he cautioned, "it's a sneak peek, a chance for you to get the feel of it. About three miles down is a turnoff that will loop back up here, so I expect to see you all in an hour. This is only the appetizer. Tomorrow is the main course." The steel in his voice brooked no argument.

Tomorrow, Shane echoed, feeling a sudden prick of urgency. Tomorrow Todd would be one day closer to a life in prison. Would Shane be any nearer to proving him innocent?

He spotted Ackerman taking pictures of the assembled racers as they strapped on helmets and headed down the trail. They were taking the trip in order of team captain's last name, so Shane had time before he and Gleeson had their turn. A few minutes to ask some questions, find out who knew Ellen Brown.

He saw that Betsy had taken Ackerman by the elbow and drawn him a few paces away from the crowd. Moving closer, Shane brushed by Kelly.

She gave him a close look. "Excited about the course?"

"Yeah, itching to take it on. Was that your aunt I saw in camp?"

"Yes, she's come to watch Charlie during the race events."

Shane nodded. "He'll like that, I'm sure."

She didn't answer, and the silence between them thickened.

He flicked a glance at Ackerman. Betsy was gesticulating to him angrily. "Seems like those two are having some trouble."

Kelly followed his gaze. "Looks that way." She hesitated for a moment before putting a hand on his arm, the fingers squeezing slightly. "Shane, just focus on the race. It's a dangerous course. If your mind is somewhere else…"

"What's the matter, Kell? You're afraid I'll get hurt? I'm practically a superhero on a bike. Without the cape, of course." He tried for a light and flirty tone, the old Shane Mason who loved a good laugh and kept all the darkness bottled up tight.

She read the tone underneath and removed her hand. "I don't want anyone to get hurt."

Just her professional side talking. Nothing more.

The withdrawal was bigger than just her hand pulling away. He saw the first racer head down the trail. "I'll do what I came here to do." He felt her eyes following him as he headed toward his bike.

Gleeson was already putting on his own helmet and rolling his bike toward the start. Up ahead, coppery braid trailing down her back, Betsy's voice rose in anger as Shane approached.

"That's just fine, isn't it? I've done everything for you."

Ackerman saw Shane coming and tried for a smile, at the same time holding up a calming hand to Betsy. "We'll talk later."

"No, we won't," she snapped, pulling away from him and storming toward the bikes.

"Women," Ackerman said, a sheepish grin on his face.

"Guess she's immune to your charm."

He shrugged. "A tiff. It will blow over."

Some tiff. He thought about asking Ackerman about the picture of Olivia and Betsy. No, he decided. He'd ask Betsy himself. She might be more likely to let drop some details that he could use about what had happened the year before. Maybe he'd luck out, and she'd have an old phone number for Ellen. Perhaps they'd been pals.

Shane moved toward his bike, stepping out of the way as Betsy pedaled past, her lips drawn tight, eyes narrowed.

"Hang on, Betsy. That's..."

She zoomed by him and headed down the course. He trotted to a spot where he could watch her descent. It was an easy slope for the first ten yards, but just before the turn, the trail dropped off sharply. Betsy eased back until she was actually crouched behind her bicycle seat, her weight over the rear wheel. It was clear she was a good rider.

He continued to watch, arms folded. A murmur went through the crowd as the bike suddenly wobbled and the rear wheel collapsed on itself. There was a collective gasp from the onlookers as Betsy went down. The last thing he saw was the bike tipping over the cliff side and Betsy hurtling through the air, her braid catching the light as she spun.

His legs moved of their own accord as he ran down the trail, slipping on a patch of loose rock. Out of the corner of his eye he saw Ackerman following and Kelly behind him. In a rush of loose earth, his heart beating rapidly, Shane made his way down.

Sliding to a stop at the turn, he looked over the side. The battered bike was a few yards down, caught on a rock, one of the wheels still turning crookedly. He ran to it, searching behind the shrubs and rocks for any sign of her.

"Where's Betsy?" Ackerman panted as he scrambled down next to Shane.

"She's up here," Kelly called from above.

Ackerman made it back up to the trail first, and they both arrived breathless at the spot where Betsy lay, behind a screen of rock. Kelly knelt next to her, asking questions and running her fingers gently along Betsy's neck, arms and legs.

"Thank goodness she didn't go over the side with the bike," Ackerman panted.

Betsy's nose was bleeding, and her face was crusted with dirt. "Let go," she snapped, trying to move out of Kelly's grasp.

"I need to check you over," Kelly said soothingly.

"I'm fine," Betsy said, trying to rise. "Leave me alone."

Kelly held Betsy in place. "You will lie still here until we see how bad your injuries are. Don't move until I tell you."

Something in Kelly's tone must have convinced Betsy because she closed her eyes and lay still, answering Kelly's questions in clipped syllables.

Ackerman knelt next to her and tried to take her hand, but she pulled it away.

Kelly shot him a look. "I need her to calm down now. Could you wait over there?"

Ackerman held up his hands and backed away. Martin Chenko barreled down the path, a radio clutched in his hand. "How is she? What happened? It was just a trial."

Kelly stopped his rush of questions. "I don't think anything is broken. I'm concerned about a head injury." She pulled a section of gauze from her backpack and pressed it to Betsy's wound. "We should immobilize her and get her to the hospital for a CT scan."

Betsy started to protest loudly.

Relieved that Betsy appeared to be at least conscious, Shane went back to the edge and climbed down to the bike. He had only a moment before Gleeson joined him.

"Bad way to start a race. Makes you wonder if it's worth it."

Gleeson had not seen the wheel collapse in on itself. Shane started to look closely at the bike, but a swarm of racers interrupted his examination. Several offered to help carry the bike up to the top, while another group headed for Betsy to offer words of encouragement. Gwen was among them, her face unreadable.

Shane stepped aside as Gleeson and the racers pulled the bike out. He made his way back to Kelly, his nerves prickling. He caught Kelly's eye, and hers widened just a fraction.

The bond between them must not be completely broken because he could see that she got his message loud and clear: something isn't right.

There was a flicker of alarm on her face, but it was nothing compared to the instincts roaring inside him.

SIX

Tearing her gaze away from Shane, Kelly eyed her patient. Betsy was sitting up now, against Kelly's wishes.

"I'm fine. I didn't hit my head and I'm not going to the hospital. A hot shower is all I need."

"Betsy," Chenko said. "Be a good girl now. Do what you're told."

"I've taken worse tumbles than this. I…"

He raised his voice a fraction to stop her from arguing. "Listen to me. If you continue and drop dead from a concussion, I'll have to call off the race. You don't want me to have to do that, do you? All the money I've put into this? All these racers disappointed?" There was an edge in his tone.

Something crossed Betsy's face for a moment, but Kelly could not decipher it. Betsy opened her mouth to answer and then closed it. After a moment she nodded. "Okay. I'll go for a scan but I'm not going on a stretcher, and I'll be ready to start tomorrow."

Chenko nodded. "Of course. We'll find you a new bike and you'll be tearing up the trails again tomorrow." He turned to Kelly. "Didn't think you'd be called upon already, did you?"

"I'm glad to be here to help. I'll ride with her to the hospital."

"Thank you. I'll get this chaos back in order. Devin," he called. "I'm going to need your help. Get the racers down the trail. Tell them they can walk it; no riding until it dries up some more."

"I'll drive, in case Kelly needs a hand," Shane called out.

Kelly caught the look of surprise on Chenko's face and Devin's narrowed eyes. "I should go with her," Devin said.

"No," Betsy hissed, groaning as Kelly and Shane helped her to her feet. "I don't want you to come."

He looked as though he'd been slapped.

Soon they had her loaded into the backseat. Shane eased the car to the main road as gently as he could, while Kelly sat with Betsy. She did not complain as they jostled along, but the rough terrain must have aggravated her bruised body.

"Are you okay, Betsy?" Kelly asked.

"Fine." She pressed her lips together and closed her eyes.

Kelly had phoned ahead, and fortunately the small medical center forty miles away was equipped to do a CT scan and a complete exam. The miles passed in slow motion, cliffs and grassland blurring together against the blue sky in what seemed a never-ending picture.

Kelly felt her stomach tighten, remembering the look on Shane's face. It had been a long time since she'd felt the instant emotional connection they used to enjoy all the time. Not long ago they could finish each other's sentences. She'd been able to detect somber moods in his tiniest inflection. They had shared more good times and unrestrained joy than she'd ever experienced in her life, but she'd always sensed there was a part of him—something from his past, a soul secret—that he had not shared with her. It had taken her until just that moment to realize that she hadn't pressed him because of her own dark past.

She recalled in vivid detail the night she'd run. A wild seventeen-year-old, she'd begged her then-boyfriend for a ride, the alcohol making her reckless as the hot South Dakota cliffs that vanished into the rearview mirror. If they hadn't stopped for gas, if her uncle Bill hadn't called one last time. If she hadn't felt the Lord urging her to turn around and go home.

She controlled a shudder. It was the narrowest of choices that separated her from the life that imprisoned her sister and controlled her mother for most of their childhood. The decision she'd made at that dirty gas station to go back home had saved her life. Maybe one simple choice like that would bring Rose back again, too.

Please, God. Bring Rose home.

Kelly refocused on Shane. Right now, though he was outwardly calm, she could read the tension in his jaw. He looked in the rearview mirror from time to time, but he did not make eye contact with her. Clearly, whatever it was, he did not want to discuss it with Betsy in the back.

His bangs hung in his face, lending him the roguish air that had always thrilled her. He was fearless about nearly everything, but something was weighing on him right now, and there was no way to identify it until they reached their destination.

An hour of relative silence passed, broken only by Kelly's questions to Betsy to check for altered consciousness, and an occasional comment from Shane. With a profound sense of relief, they pulled into the clinic and met the waiting medics. They loaded Betsy on a stretcher in spite of her protests and took her for a scan.

Kelly sagged, feeling the tension ebb for the first time since she'd watched as Betsy had flown off her bike.

Shane caught her arm and pulled her to his side. "Let me buy you a cup of coffee. We need to talk."

She didn't argue. Pulled against his muscled arm, she let herself be guided along. They found a cafeteria, complete with bad coffee, and made their way to a small courtyard, empty except for an orderly reading a newspaper in the far corner. They sat at a table near a scraggly yucca plant.

Sliding into a chair, she felt her senses returning to normal. "What's going on?" she demanded before the first sip.

He stared at her. "I'm not sure where to begin."

She waited, watching his eyes flicker in thought, like ocean water rippled by a strong current.

He cleared his throat. "I don't think Betsy's crash was an accident."

Kelly gulped the coffee and burned her tongue. "How do you figure that? Is it part of your theory about Ackerman?"

"I'm not sure."

Kelly felt competing emotions swirl inside her. On the one hand, she wanted to reach out and shake the paranoia out of Shane, but there was something in his face that prevented her from moving. "Tell me what you think happened."

"I only got a split-second look at the bike before they hauled it away."

"And?"

"I think some of the spokes might have been partially cut."

"Cut?" She gaped. "But that couldn't happen. Everyone inspects their equipment before the race. There's no way Betsy would have missed that."

He hesitated. "First off, if the spokes were weakened, but not completely severed, she might not have. But we all went over our bikes back in camp. Then they were parked together while we looked at the course." He paused. "Un-attended."

She shook her head. "That's insane. No one would do that. With all those people watching?"

His eyes narrowed, the bright blue a startling contrast in his tanned face. "Someone did."

She tried another tack. "Any racer worth their salt would check their bike again before race time."

"You saw for yourself—Betsy was arguing with Acker-man."

"But…"

"She was angry. She grabbed the bike and took off."

Kelly sat back in her chair. He was clearly not going to listen to reason. "Okay. If you're right, then call the police."

"I thought about it, but that would end the race. Every-one would scatter, and I'd never find Ellen Brown."

Kelly couldn't stop herself. She reached out and took his hand. "There's no certainty that Ellen would tell you any-thing different than she told the police, even if you did find her. Listen to yourself, Shane. You're not making any sense. Your need to help your brother is blinding you to reality."

For a moment, his long fingers tightened in hers, cup-ping their hands together. Then he pulled away and fixed his blazing eyes on hers. "I have to see this thing through. It's the only way to save Todd. I've got to."

"I know you want to help him…"

He slapped a hand on the table. "Listen, Kelly, I'm not going to lose a brother, not again."

She frowned. Again? "What do you mean?"

He took a drink of coffee and shook his head. "Nothing. I'm not going to involve the police just now."

"Well, what are you going to do? If you think the bike was tampered with, you have an obligation to say so. Other people could be hurt, and you can't ignore that."

"I won't. I'm going to confront Ackerman and examine the bike. We'll be able to see if the spokes were weakened." He took her hand again and pressed his rough cheek into her palm, planting a soft kiss on the sensitive flesh. "I'm sorry I've brought you into all this, Kell. But will you believe me now? Will you take Charlie and get out of here before you get hurt?"

She stared into his face and saw his earnest plea. Her fingers tingled where his chin rested there. She slowly pulled her hands away. "I'll have to see it for myself."

He smiled. "Yes, ma'am."

She shook her head to clear it. "Hang on. I'm not saying I believe any of this, but for the sake of argument, how would sabotaging Besty's bike serve any purpose at all?"

He heaved a sigh and rolled the cup between his palms, as though fighting off a chill.

"Shane? What aren't you telling me?"

Unexpectedly his face softened into a wistful smile. "How can you tell I'm holding something back?"

"It's the same look Charlie gives me when he's filled his pockets from the cookie jar."

He laughed. "You know, you're a real good mom."

The comment stunned her for a moment. He'd told her once that his mother was the greatest woman he had ever known. She wondered why sadness shimmered in his eyes when he'd said it. "Thank you." She fiddled with her own cup to buy herself a moment, unable to stop the angry thought that rose up in her mind. If he thought she was great mother material, why had he run? Why had he tossed her heart away and taken off when she'd decided to raise Charlie? He didn't have to sign on to be a father, but abandoning her had been a coward's choice. She wanted to lash out, but it was not the time. She cleared her throat.

"So why do you think someone would try to sabotage Betsy's bike?"

"I don't," he said, crushing the empty cup in his palm. "The bike was mine. She took it by mistake."

Shane watched Kelly pace the small courtyard, making various calls back to camp to report on Betsy's condition. The doctor confirmed that Betsy was indeed fine, bruised and banged up, but otherwise okay. Though he recommended strongly that she skip the race the following day, his shrug told them he realized the futility of forbidding Betsy from any such activity.

It was several hours before she was released and they began the car drive back. Kelly avoided looking at Shane, and he could tell he'd upset her with his revelation. Betsy sat in sullen silence in the backseat. Shane eased into some small talk, which got only one-word answers. He went for a more direct approach.

"So Betsy, how did you meet Ackerman?"

She blinked. "Why do you want to know?"

"Just curious."

Betsy looked out the window as she answered. "He came to a coffee shop where I worked last year, and I heard him talking about the race. I sort of tagged along and volunteered to help out, got to know everyone."

"What was the last race like? Heard they had a horseback-riding event."

She looked at him sharply. "Yes, but that didn't last long."

"Why? I could go for some riding."

She shrugged and fingered the bandage on her brow.

Shane decided to go for broke. "I heard there was a girl murdered last year—someone connected to the race."

Betsy's expression did not change, but something in her eyes flickered. "That was bad, but it wasn't a racer. The woman was supplying horses for us and someone murdered her. No connection really. Haven't lost anyone in the race yet."

Kelly piped up. "I was reading through the files from last year's medic. He noted that a girl was hospitalized. Her name was Ellen, I think."

Shane barely concealed his surprise. Kelly must have looked up Ellen's name. Was she starting to believe him?

"Ellen got sick." Betsy closed her eyes.

Shane tried hard for a nonchalant tone. "Do you still keep in contact with her?"

"No. I never liked her much. She was a liar. I'm just going to take a nap now. Thanks for driving me, by the way."

Shane caught Kelly's eye, but they didn't speak. Betsy hadn't confirmed anything new, though Shane hadn't been aware that Ellen had been hospitalized, but that went with the territory in the risky business of racing. The hostility made sense, too, if Ellen was interested in Ackerman. In her statement to the police, Ellen claimed she was with Ackerman in his trailer the night Olivia was killed.

His mind drifted back to the bike. He hadn't seen Ackerman near it, but the guy had been wandering all over, taking pictures. It would only have taken a moment. Pretend to drop something. Lean over and snip. All done and no one would be the wiser. When the rider leaned his or her weight over the rear wheel, collapse was inevitable. What excited him most was that if Ackerman wanted him gone, that meant he was getting nervous and maybe, just maybe, Shane was getting closer to the truth that would set his brother free.

The journey back seemed to take twice as long. It was nearly dark when they arrived. Ackerman materialized at the car door with Chenko and Gwen. They peppered Betsy with questions. The woman seemed to be more tired than angry now. She even managed a wan smile. "I'm fine. Doc says I've got a hard head. I'm cleared to race tomorrow."

Chenko shot a look at Kelly, who confirmed Betsy's statement with a nod.

"Why don't we wait and see how you're feeling?" Chenko said. "I don't want any more accidents."

Betsy opened her mouth to retort, but Gwen put an arm around her and led her away toward their trailer. Ackerman started to follow when Shane stopped him.

"I need to tell you something."

Ackerman smiled. "Gleeson figured out that Betsy took your bike by mistake. Sorry about that. We'll fix you up with a new one."

"That's not it. The crash wasn't an accident. Someone tampered with the spokes."

Both Chenko and Ackerman stared at him. "Are you kidding?" Ackerman managed.

"No, I wish I was."

"Look, Matthews," Chenko said. "I figured you were overtired when you made that accusation about someone breaking into your cabin. Now you've got some theory that there's a villain afoot trying to sabotage my race?"

Shane shook his head. "Not the race. Just me—someone wants to put me out of commission."

Ackerman folded his arms. "Now why would anyone want to do that?"

"I don't know."

"This is ludicrous," Ackerman said angrily, taking a step forward. "You're a complete nutcase."

Shane straightened, his tall frame topping Ackerman's by several inches. "I don't think so."

Chenko stepped between the two men. "All right, there's

an easy way to put this to bed. We'll take a look at the bike. If the spokes were damaged on purpose, we'll be able to tell in a matter of minutes. Where is it?"

Ackerman's eyes didn't move from Shane's face. "In the trailer, hooked up to the back of the truck. I drove it back here myself. It's parked over there." He jerked a thumb toward a vehicle parked in a pool of light cast by the lodge.

"Fine then. Let's go," Chenko said.

Shane followed Chenko. Ackerman held back to walk with Kelly. Shane could hear the conversation, even though they kept it low.

"What's up with that guy?" Ackerman said. "He's nuts."

"Let's see what the bike looks like before we decide anything like that," Kelly said.

Her comment warmed him. At least she wasn't going to trash him in front of Ackerman. Of course, he knew she probably thought he was crazy, maddened by worry for his brother. He quickened his pace. In a few more minutes they would know for sure.

Gleeson emerged from the shadows, holding a sandwich. "What's going on?"

"We're going to take a look at Shane's bike. He believes it was tampered with."

Gleeson didn't answer. Shane thought the reaction was strange, but he did not have time to grill his partner further. They came to the trailer, covered by a yellow tarp.

"I can't believe we're entertaining this wacko's conspiracy theories," Ackerman said.

"Fact finding," Chenko snapped. "That's how you problem-solve."

Shane took hold of the tarp and pulled it back. All four of them stared into the trailer.

It was Gleeson who finally broke the silence with a low whistle. "That's unexpected."

Not entirely, Shane thought, eyes roving the empty space. *If I tampered with the bike, I'd get rid of it, too.*

SEVEN

Kelly watched in dismay as Shane rounded on Devin.

"Where's the bike? What did you do with it?"

Devin fisted his hands on his hips. "I didn't do anything. It was here. Someone must have taken it. Gleeson, do you know anything about this?"

Gleeson shrugged. "Nah. I'm just here to race. Didn't see anyone make off with it."

Chenko sighed, his face etched with fatigue. "All right. We'll ask about it in the morning. I'm sure it just got parked somewhere, or a few helpful people are trying to repair it. For now," he fixed eyes on Shane, "I don't want to hear you going around accusing people of sabotage. I can't stand that kind of bad PR, and I'd just as soon kick you out as let you do any damage. I've worked for years to make this race the prestigious event that it is, and I won't have you messing that up. Do you understand me, Mr. Matthews?"

Kelly held her breath, waiting for Shane's response. He was livid; she could tell by the set of his broad shoulders. She moved near and put a hand on his shoulder, feeling the tension that lay there like a coiled snake. "Shane, leave it for now. Let's go get something to eat. I want to check in on Charlie, too. Walk me to my trailer?"

Chenko shook his head. "Not until I get an answer from

him. Right now you have exactly zero proof that anything improper has happened. Mr. Matthews, do I have your word that you won't start spreading rumors?"

"You have my word."

Shane turned and followed Kelly. She caught the smile on Devin's face, a smile of satisfaction. And triumph.

She saw that Chenko noticed it, too. Suddenly he looked much older than he was. Shane followed her in silence. Before they went inside the trailer, she stopped him. "I don't want Charlie to overhear anything that might upset him."

Shane still did not respond. The darkness made it impossible to read his expression, but his silence made her more uncomfortable by the minute. "I'm sure the bike was just moved somewhere else. We can find it in the morning, and then we'll know for sure."

He blinked. "What does your gut tell you right now?"

She shrugged, moving to go inside.

He took her arm and turned her to him. Her heart hammered as she drew close, and the urge to trace the contours of his face nearly overpowered her.

"Do you think I'm telling the truth?" he whispered.

The past came rushing back to her. The day she held Charlie and told him her decision.

I'm going to raise him.

The haunted look in his eyes as he'd stared at the child. *I can't,* he'd said. *I love you, but I can't. I'm sorry.*

And that was that.

Anger and hurt swirled together, as strong and bitter as the day he'd left. Did she believe him? She wanted to lash out, to hurt him just as he'd hurt her so deeply.

"Yes," she found herself saying, surprised by her own words. "I don't know why, but I do believe you."

His smile caught a sliver of moonlight, turning his face

suddenly radiant. He pulled her close, into a gentle embrace. "Thank you."

She relaxed into it for a moment, his warmth pressing away the coolness of the night. It was bittersweet, and she would not allow herself to be swept up into a storm of emotion that would bring nothing but pain again. She pushed away. "You're welcome. And before you ask, there was no contact information on past racers, just a list of dates of participation. It's all been shredded, and even if it wasn't, I couldn't give it to you."

Though his heart sank, he managed a smile. "I appreciate it anyway."

"Come in and say hello to Aunt Jean. We can make some sandwiches."

He followed her up. Kelly kissed her aunt on the cheek and swept Charlie into a tight embrace, blowing a raspberry onto his neck. He giggled and squirmed until she put him down. Shane greeted Aunt Jean warmly, but he was slightly guarded, no doubt feeling awkward about seeing her again after he'd broken things off with Kelly.

"How is that poor gal who took a spill?" Aunt Jean asked, scooping Paddy Paws into her lap and stroking the bony cat.

"She'll be okay," Kelly said. Shane exchanged a look with her. He didn't want to involve her aunt in his sabotage theories, and that was just fine with Kelly. Kelly inhaled the tangy scent of onions and garlic. "What's cooking?"

Aunt Jean waved a hand. "Needed something to do while Charlie was napping so I made chili. Would have made pie, but your cupboards are a little lean." She bustled into the tiny kitchen and dished them all up a bowl.

Charlie picked at his and asked to be excused to play. He climbed onto the bed to make roads and tunnels in the sheets. Kelly watched him, delighted afresh with his ability to find joy in the simplest things. She felt her aunt's gaze.

"I can't believe he's going to be four. Rose will hardly recognize him," Kelly said. "She tried to talk to him on the phone a few months back, but he was too shy to talk."

"Honey…" Aunt Jean's words trailed off.

Something akin to worry stirred in Kelly's stomach. "What is it?"

Jean darted a look at Shane and toyed with her napkin.

He wiped his mouth. "Thank you for the chili," he said. "I think I'd better be going."

Jean smiled but did not try to dissuade him from leaving. It made Kelly's worry flare up in earnest as she walked Shane to the door.

He touched her hand. "Everything okay?" he whispered.

"I'm not sure." She shot a worried glance at Aunt Jean, who was answering her satellite phone. "You're not going to do anything rash about this bike-tampering business, are you?"

He gave her a roguish grin. "Me? Rash? When was the last time I did anything rash?"

"The day your car wouldn't start, so you drove your buddy's tractor to pick me up for a date."

They both laughed.

"Well, you have to admit you'd never rode in style like that before, had you?" Shane asked.

"No," she said, shaking her head. "I hadn't."

They fell into an awkward silence as the reality of their relationship intruded. Those days were past. Long past. "Anyway, I'll see you in the morning."

Shane nodded and reached for the door when Aunt Jean came toward them. The look on her face was a ghastly mixture of fear and disbelief. She stumbled slightly and Shane reached for her arm, supporting her back to the kitchen chair.

Kelly grabbed her hand, which was cold to the touch and shaking. "What's going on? Please tell me."

Aunt Jean shot a look at Charlie to make sure he was still engrossed in his car game. "Your Uncle Bill—he's been searching everywhere for Rose, you know."

"I know. Did he hear something?"

She nodded. "He's got contacts, and he put out the word to police departments, private investigators—" She paused. "Hospitals."

"He found her? Aunt Jean, please tell me. Did he find her?" Kelly's heart thundered so loud in her ears, she wondered if they could all hear it.

"It might not be true."

"What?"

Jean looked from Shane to Kelly to Shane again.

"Would it be easier if I left?" Shane asked.

She shook her head and lowered her voice to a whisper. Both Shane and Kelly leaned close to hear. "Honey, the police found a body that matches the description of your sister. Uncle Bill is driving up tomorrow to…to make an identification."

Kelly blinked. Slowly her eyes traveled to Charlie, talking happily to himself about cars and vacations and inviting imaginary people to his birthday party. "So…Rose is… dead?"

Jean pressed her lips together as her eyes filled with tears.

Kelly felt Shane's arm around her, leading her to a chair. "It's not certain," he said. "You won't know for sure until your uncle contacts you."

But Kelly knew.

From the moment her twin had left home permanently at age eighteen, fleeing the consequences of her alcoholism, Kelly had known deep down that she would not share a life with her sister again. There were strained phone calls, requests for money, occasional texts about a new job or boyfriend, but Rose had cut her ties to home, just as Kelly had almost done. Kelly remembered one particularly worrying call several years back about a man who was treating her badly, then Rose refused to speak about it again. After that the contact was erratic and unpredictable. Though their mother had finally gotten clean near the end of her life, Rose had learned the lesson too well by then. Anger, resentment, rejection, fear, sorrow. They were all easier to manage with a bottle of whiskey and a half-dozen beers.

Anger bubbled inside. *How come my sister couldn't beat it, Lord?*

Kelly's mother was dead. Now her sister. They were both gone. She'd never met her father. Even the woman sitting across from her was not her real aunt, just a dear family friend who'd taken on the role of family. She had Uncle Bill and Charlie. She looked at the child again, so fresh-faced and sweet. How could Rose have left him?

The truth was a bitter venom flowing through her veins. Charlie's mother was dead.

And Kelly was all he had left.

Shane stayed for a while, bringing them both glasses of water and helping Charlie make a gas station out of a tissue box. It was all he could think of to do. Kelly's face was dead white, and though she did not cry, neither would she talk about the feelings reflected in her eyes.

When he finally left, promising to come back if they needed anything at all, he found himself unable to return to his trailer. Instead, he went for a run along the moonlit trail, his feet moving faster and faster until his breath rasped out of him.

He wanted to wrap Kelly up and take her away from this

place, to run until they found a place far from their past, from the sorrow that continued to pile brick upon brick until it threatened to blot out the sunlight. He was inexplicably angry that Rose was probably dead. Shane knew that he deserved the despair that had grown to be a part of him, but Kelly did not. It was not fair.

She'd made brave choices, overcoming her wild youth, putting herself through nursing school, taking in her sister's child. She was innocent, and she did not deserve the sorrow raining down on her.

"She doesn't deserve it!" he shouted at the cloud-patterned darkness. "Do You hear me? She doesn't deserve it, and neither does Charlie." His shout echoed back to him, and he was surprised to feel moisture on his cheeks—tears that he did not understand fell to the damp earth under his feet. A thought struck him with all the force of a clenched fist. Staggering to a stop, pulse pounding, he realized that he was not thinking just of Kelly and Charlie, but of another innocent, a small boy whom God had snatched away in the blink of an eye.

"I'll never be free," he said to the silent cliffs. "I'll never be free of it."

He wondered suddenly if he would lose his brother, Todd, just as swiftly. The evidence would convict him, and nothing Shane did snooping around this race and baiting Ackerman would make any difference at all. He had as much chance of changing the course of events as he had changing the direction of the wind that buffeted leaves against his face.

No. His hands balled into fists, jaw clenched. *I'll save him.*

He repeated the words over and over as he slowly looped back to camp, sweat beading on his face in spite of the chilly evening. The campground became visible, nestled in the thicket of trees that surrounded it. The property all around was made up of acres of rocky ground, low hills, dense shrubbery and twisted canyons.

He thought he saw movement to his left, in the bushes. The wind.

He slowed to a walk and continued on. Another flicker in the branches. A coyote?

Skin prickling on the back of his neck, he continued walking, forcing himself not to look. Ahead was an outcropping of rock that cast dark shadows across the moonlit ground. Shane passed it and immediately turned, silently scrambled up the rock and peered over the top.

The movement was too big for an animal, he realized. A tiny flicker of light appeared and then vanished. The beam of a small flashlight.

He waited, hardly daring to breathe as the figure moved toward the trail. One more minute and it would emerge.

A cloud blotted out the moonlight just as the prowler stepped onto the path, pocketing the flashlight.

Gleeson. Silver hair luminous against the darkness.

Shane didn't wait any longer. He jumped down. "Hey," he called.

Gleeson jerked, tensing for a moment before he relaxed. "You scared me."

"What are you doing here?"

Gleeson cocked his head, jamming his hands into the pockets of his jeans. "What are *you* doing here?"

"Out for a run," Shane said.

"Me, too, but I run slower than you."

Shane considered whether or not to force a confrontation. He gestured to the flashlight tucked into Gleeson's pocket. "Always run with that?"

He smiled. "Smart, isn't it? You never know when you'll

need a flashlight. Thought I saw a mountain lion. Good thing I was wrong."

Shane joined Gleeson as they walked the path back to the campground. He didn't believe Gleeson's story for a moment, but he had no reason to suspect the man of wrong-doing. Did everyone in camp have something to hide?

"So you really think someone messed with your bike?"

Shane nodded.

"Why would they do that?"

"I don't know."

Gleeson eyed him. "You sure?"

Shane stopped. "What's that supposed to mean?"

"Nothing—it's just that maybe you've got an ulterior motive in being here. Maybe you're here to stir up trouble, and somebody wants to prevent you from doing that."

The two eyed each other silently until Shane spoke. "Or maybe someone here has a guilty conscience."

Gleeson's eyes narrowed slightly. "Who doesn't?" He continued on a few paces. "Strange that the bike is missing, the one that would prove or disprove your sabotage story."

"Very strange. Do you have any idea where it might be?"

"No. I'd tell you if I did. We're partners, right?"

As they approached the campground, Shane wondered. Partners? Or enemies?

The day finally caught up with Shane, and his legs felt like lead as he walked toward his trailer. Gleeson was lying—he knew that. Maybe he'd cut the spokes himself, but how would he benefit from Shane getting hurt—or worse? Had Ackerman figured out Shane's real motive and paid Gleeson to get rid of him?

He was so deep in thought, he almost didn't see her at first. Kelly sat on the step to her trailer with Paddy Paws on her lap, both of them motionless, except for the stroking of her fingers on the cat's fur. She didn't seem to notice his approach, her eyes riveted to a spot on the ground.

"Hey, Kell," he said softly.

She looked up, but there was no light in her face, none of the sparkling vivacity that he loved in her. He gave the cat a scratch behind the ears. "Remember me, cat? We took a swim together, only I did all the paddling." He eased onto the step next to Kelly. A new veil of clouds danced across the moon. "We might get some rain soon."

She didn't answer.

Bring up the weather. Smooth, Shane. He remembered a time when he could talk to her about anything. Well, almost anything.

"News?" he asked.

She shook her head.

He sighed. "If there's anything I can do—anything at all, I hope you'll tell me."

She gave him a quick look and caught her lip between her teeth. "I just keep sitting here thinking that it might really be over and feeling guilty because…"

"Why would you feel guilty about any of this?"

She got up, the cat cradled in her arms, and walked aimlessly. He followed. "Tell me, Kell. Why would you feel like this was your fault in any way?"

She looked at him, eyes brimming, and he was struck again by how beautiful she was. She had always been the most exquisite woman he had ever laid eyes on. And what he knew about the sterling quality of her character made her even more breathtaking in his eyes. He pressed on. "Talk to me."

She shook her head and one tear slipped down her cheek. "I never believed in Rose."

"What do you mean?"

"She told me so many times she'd get sober, find a steady

job. And then she had Charlie." Kelly paced back and forth. "She had a child, a perfect little boy. If that isn't reason enough to change, then nothing is."

"What are you saying?"

"I'm saying that deep down in my heart, I never believed she would really beat it." She looked at him full-on then. "I spent so many years praying that my mother would. She did, you know. Well, I guess you probably didn't know that, but my mother did get clean. She was murdered, and it was made to look like an OD. My uncle almost died bringing the guy to justice."

He cringed. A bombshell truth, and he hadn't even known about it.

"So you had reasons for worrying that your sister wouldn't straighten out. Good reasons. No guilt in that."

"Maybe if I had had more faith, if I had trusted that the Lord would bring her home…"

He touched her shoulder and squeezed. "This isn't about you or the Lord. Rose made her own choices, and now…"

"And now my sister is dead."

Shane didn't get a chance to respond. They were both startled by a thunk. Whirling, Shane saw Gwen standing a few feet away, a look of horror on her face, a basket of spilled laundry at her feet.

EIGHT

"What did you say?" she whispered. "Your sister is dead?"

Kelly appeared too startled to answer.

"We're not certain," Shane said. "Did you know Rose?"

Gwen's eyes shifted from Shane to Kelly. "No, no. I don't know her. It startled me, is all. I'm sorry. I didn't mean to eavesdrop."

Kelly took a step closer. "Gwen, I feel like you're not telling me something. Why are you so interested in my sister? And Charlie?"

She bent over and began shoveling the laundry back into the basket. "No reason. I felt bad when I heard you say that about your sister. I was thinking about the little boy and how he wouldn't have his mother. I'm sorry. I didn't mean to pry."

Kelly frowned at her. She was about to press the woman further, but Shane sensed that Gwen was ready to bolt.

He gave her a friendly smile. "This your first race?"

She nodded, looking slightly more relaxed. "My cousin talked me into it. I watched a little of the race last year, and I figured I could manage it."

"A nice group of people, don't you think? Betsy must have friends here since she helped out last year."

She didn't answer.

"Did you ever get to meet a gal from last year's race? A friend of Betsy's, I think. Ellen Brown. A blonde…"

It was impossible to tell in the gloom, but he thought he saw a flitter of something in her face at the mention of the name.

"No. I don't think I ever met her."

"Gwen…" Kelly started to say, but the woman had already turned and hurried away.

Kelly stared at Shane. "What do you make of that?"

He following the departing figure with his eyes. "Strange."

"I feel somehow as if she's connected to my sister, but she couldn't be, could she?"

"Certainly not that she's going to admit to."

Kelly chewed her lip, nuzzling Paddy under her chin. "I get the oddest feeling from her. Am I imagining things?"

He could find no words. Though he tried his best to think of comforting things to say, he came up with nothing. She said goodnight and closed the door. He found his way back to his own trailer and fixed himself a sandwich that he didn't really taste.

Gleeson, Gwen, Betsy, Ackerman, Chenko. They all raced around in his mind, pulling his thoughts in different directions. In spite of the confusion, one face rose to the top.

Kelly.

Tomorrow the race would start in earnest. Whoever had tried to sideline him today would have another chance soon. And tomorrow, Kelly would find out if her sister Rose was dead or alive.

He wished he had a prayer to offer to ease the anguish in her heart, but he had nothing to give God but rage and resentment.

Tomorrow he would be on his own to face whatever was in store for him.

* * *

Kelly awoke before sunup, drenched in sweat. Had the phone rung? She listened, heart pounding. No. It was just in her dream.

She dragged herself out of bed, careful not to wake Charlie, and went to fix some coffee. Aunt Jean was already up, hands folded across her lap, lost in thought.

"Did you get any sleep?" Kelly whispered.

"Not much, honey. You?"

Kelly sank down with a sigh into the chair across from her. "I'm scared."

"Me, too."

"I prayed and prayed."

"Same here." Jean reached over and gripped Kelly's hand. "We'll get through this. I'm praying the Lord didn't call Rosie home, not while her little boy needs her, but if He did…"

"If He did…" Kelly felt her eyes fill, so she forced a deep breath. "I'll be as good a parent to Charlie as I can."

"I know."

Kelly thought about how she would tell Charlie that his mother had died. The little boy had asked a few times who his father was, but Kelly could honestly say she did not know. Rose had never shared that information, and now Kelly might never get the chance to ask. Turning away, she looked at the clock. Six fifteen. The racers would have a light breakfast at 7:30 and head to the site. The mountain-biking event was set to kick off at 9:00 and last until after sunset. She would be there, checking in on the racers, on standby for any injuries.

She noticed a tray with two coffees, juice and a plateful of bagels.

"Where did that come from?"

"It was on the doorstep when I got up, along with a note."
Aunt Jean pointed to a scrap on the counter.

Thought you might want to have breakfast in your trailer.
Let me know if you need anything. S

Kelly sighed. It was just the sort of thing Shane would
do, had done often in the time they were together. Once he'd
even had a pizza and two dozen roses delivered to her apart-
ment during an intense cram session before her chemistry
exam. She felt Jean's eyes on her.

"So where exactly do you and Shane stand?" she asked,
taking the coffee Kelly handed her.

"Nowhere."

She eyed the bagels. "He must think highly of you."

"Not highly enough to stay." Kelly picked at a bagel.
"As soon as I took Charlie in, he ran. He never wanted to
be a father. I knew that, but I thought…I imagined…never
mind."

Charlie padded sleepily into the kitchen and climbed up
to the table. Both Aunt Jean and Kelly kissed him.

"So you're going to stay with Aunt Jean today, Charlie,
while I go to work. Will you be a good boy for her?"

He nodded solemnly and sipped the orange juice.

Kelly raised an eyebrow. "And you'll call me as soon as
there's news," she whispered.

"Yes."

"Promise?"

Aunt Jean held up her fingers in a Girl Scout salute. "I
promise."

A quick shower and Kelly was in a fresh pair of pants
borrowed from Betsy. She didn't see Shane as she drove
up to the starting line with a car full of medical supplies.
Had the bike turned up anywhere, she wondered? If Shane

was right, then someone really had been trying to frighten him…or worse.

She pushed down a pang of fear. Shane could take care of himself. Most likely he'd been wrong about the spokes. Still, the feeling of unease stuck with her. She saw Shane looking closely at his bike, and Betsy, seemingly in good spirits in spite of the bandage on her face. She lost them in the crowd for a moment.

Devin appeared at her shoulder. "Hi there. Sleep okay?"

"Sure. Did you? I imagine you were worried about Betsy."

He took the lens cap off his camera. "She assured me she was okay. Hard to know what to believe sometimes," he mumbled.

"Oh?" Kelly caught the subtle current of anger in the words.

"Never mind," he said brightly. "It's race day and I've got pictures to take. Got your radio?"

"Yes." She waved the antenna at him. "Right here."

"Great. After we get them started, I can show you a great midpoint to keep an eye on the action." He snapped a picture of her before she could turn away. "Gotcha."

"Can I ask a question?"

"You can ask me anything."

Kelly leaned slightly away. "I was looking through the files, and you had a racer leave last year due to illness."

He quirked an eyebrow. "Um, yes. I remember that."

"What sort of illness was it?"

His eyebrows quirked. "Why do you want to know?"

She shrugged. "Professional curiosity. I wondered if it was something contagious, and how it was handled by the previous medic."

He thought for a moment. "I think it was a flu or something like that. She went to the hospital overnight and then decided to quit the race. Nothing too dramatic." He waved his camera. "Gotta go."

She watched him trot to the starting line and scope out a spot to catch the racers as they took off. She spotted Shane and Gleeson among the group, red helmets shining in the sunlight. Shane waved at her as Chenko climbed atop a rock, starting gun in hand.

The shot rang out and the racers surged forward in an untidy pack, clumping together along the first mile, which was relatively flat. They began to slow and spread out as they approached the descent that led to the turn where Betsy had gone down.

Her stomach tightened. She'd knew Shane would go over his new bike meticulously, filling the tires, lubing the chain, until he was satisfied that no accident would occur during the race.

She wasn't so sure. A feeling of dread clung to her and would not be shaken off. Was it her fear that Uncle Bill would return with news that Rose was dead? She shut the anxious thoughts down, busying herself checking her clipboard to make sure she had all the racers accounted for and rechecking her medical supplies for the umpteenth time.

Whatever would happen in the next few hours, she could not make it better by stewing on it.

Lord, help me take care of these racers today.

She wondered why the only racer who popped into her mind was the blue-eyed man who had broken her heart.

Shane relished the feel of being in the pack of bikers and the satisfying moment when he pulled away, establishing his place early on among the leaders. Gleeson was the third racer to start the descent and Shane kept a good five yards behind him. The first ten miles comprised a rough single-track descent. The rocky downhill required him to weight back, but not so far back that he lost traction. Wrists low on the bars, pedals even to the ground, bike in third gear. Chenko had done a good job picking the course. It took all Shane's powers of concentration to keep from wiping out. After an hour or so, the harsh downslope gradually evened out into several miles of flat grassland, which gave him time to collect his thoughts. He knew they would be headed into a wooded section next, which would be peppered with obstacles, as well.

None of the obstacles seemed to be nearly as difficult as the ones he'd already encountered. The steady motion of his feet pressing the bike forward eased him into reviewing the issues prickling at his mind. There was no info in the race files to point to Ellen Brown. Dead end there. But what about Betsy? She knew Ellen, though there was no love lost between them. Her temperament was volatile, and if he could get her talking, she just might reveal what she meant when she'd said Ellen was a liar.

He shifted to second gear as a prairie dog poked his head out of a hole to check out the racers. Ahead, the trail narrowed to a small gap, hemmed in by trees as it dropped down near the riverbed. He didn't hear the approach, but suddenly there was a biker pulling up alongside him. Surely whoever it was would fall in behind as they approached the gap.

Instead, the biker pulled forward, crowding Shane to the gravelly periphery of the path. He fought to keep the bike from slipping on the loose gravel. Betsy edged by him, so close he could see the sweat glistening on her forehead.

"Hey," he yelled. Unwilling to give in, he pushed on until both of them were hurtling toward the narrow opening. She shot him a quick look and lowered her head, driving hard on the pedals. They were only a few feet from the gap, and she showed no signs of slowing. He caught a feverish look on her face, a focus so determined it seemed to exclude everything around her.

Two feet to go, and they would smash into each other. Anger humming in his veins, Shane slowed and let Betsy by. She shot forward through the gap and disappeared into the trees. As he rolled down onto the shaded path, he wondered about the look on her face.

Betsy Falco was determined to win.

Deadly determined.

He filed the thought away as he navigated the various logs and stumps that lined the route. They were a good ten miles into the race. The river was nearly full, rushing along, a companion to him as he went. He savored the rich smell of damp earth and leaves, especially considering that the next section would take him out of the river valley and into a bone-crunching climb in a barren moonscape. Betsy and Gleeson were ahead on the trail somewhere. He wondered who would back down if they met in a similar showdown. Gleeson was tough as nails. His bearing spoke of a military background. There was a lot more to him than met the eye. Somehow, Shane knew that Gleeson had an ulterior motive in the Desert Quest, just as he did. As the miles passed, he came no closer to figuring it out.

The last few miles, the geology shifted in front of his eyes from lush and green to arid and parched. He'd ridden a relatively flat section for almost an hour, passing a racer repairing a tire and looking as tired as Shane no doubt did. Now the route began to rise quickly. It was past noon and the sunlight illuminated the jagged rocks, which shone golden. He thought about a phrase he'd heard once about the Badlands, that it was the land God forgot, but watching the rich palette of golds and browns glittering around him and the vibrant blue sky atop it all, he had an unfamiliar stirring inside—a strange feeling of awe that did not in any way fit the circumstances of his life or Kelly's at the moment. He felt something he could only identify as gratefulness, a surge of glory at being there, forging through the fantastic landscape.

He weighted forward and, as the slope grew steeper, his progress slowed until each stroke of the pedals was a great labor. The shrubs grew spotty; soon there was hardly a plant to be seen anywhere as he passed pinnacles of rock, twisted like arthritic fingers. As he stood on the pedals, grinding his way up the harsh path, the walls seemed to close in like giant stony fists, painting Shane in gloomy shadow. Ahead he could hear the occasional squeak of a laboring bike, but he could not see Betsy or Gleeson, nor could he hear any of the racers that he knew must be a couple of miles or so behind him.

He felt alone, swallowed up in this bizarre gullet of stone. A sensation pricked his neck. He scanned all sides, but saw only rock.

He didn't dare stop to listen closely and lose whatever momentum he'd managed to gain on the almost vertical climb. Ahead the trail narrowed even further, steep walls rising up on either side. He pressed on, sweat pouring down his face.

A crack sounded from above. His head snapped around, and for a moment he saw nothing. Then a rock the size of a hubcap came crashing down. There was no way to speed past it. He did the only thing he could, throwing himself off the bike and rolling himself into a ball, covering his head with both arms.

The rock hit the spot just above his head and glanced off his helmet, peppering his arms and neck with shards that cut into his skin before it continued to bounce along, until it cleared the side and careened away into the sunlit air.

He didn't take the time to catch his breath. On his feet, he tried to pinpoint where the rock had come from. They were in dangerous country. It might have been loosened by the movement of the racers passing along. That was the most plausible explanation.

But somehow that didn't satisfy the suspicion humming through his body. He walked his bike up the remaining fifty feet or so to the apex of the trail, listening carefully for any sound of falling rock. He heard nothing, so he continued on, wiping at a scrape on his forehead that now oozed blood. Even in late afternoon, even in October, the temperature was hot, and Shane found the going rough. Just before he reached the top, the click of a camera startled him. Devin Ackerman appeared over the crest.

"Come on, Matthews. Walking your bike? You've still got another eight miles to go."

Shane looked him over. He was in the perfect location to have snuck around and loosened the rock. "Rock fall."

"Really?" Ackerman cocked his head. "Didn't hear any of the racers radio that in."

"Just me," he said as he continued to push the bike.

"Bad luck, man. You seem to have a target on your back."

Shane didn't answer. *And you've got one, too, Ackerman. You just don't know it yet.*

NINE

Kelly watched as the sun set into a glorious golden pool behind the pinnacles. Darkness fell quickly, and a chill crept through the rocks. She glanced at her phone again. No messages. With a deep sigh, she kept her eyes trained on the horizon to spot the first racers. They were required to check in with her after this leg of the race, so she would be here another few hours until all fifty racers had made it back.

She looked at the leaderboard again. Each racer carried a satellite GPS that sent location based signals to the online leaderboard, which they could view in real time. Gleeson was number one, followed by another participant, then Betsy Falco and Shane. Behind them was a considerable gap, and then many racers clumped together. At least Shane was safe and moving forward, no potentially deadly accidents this time.

She suppressed a shudder, remembering Betsy hurtling through the air. And Shane was convinced the accident had been intended for him. It was crazy, too crazy to believe, but why had the bike disappeared?

A biker appeared around the last turn. Gleeson's face was a mask of concentration as he pumped toward the finish line. Crossing it, he raised a fist in victory, passed Ackerman and Chenko, and pedaled slowly over to Kelly, breathing hard.

"Great job," she told him, offering him a bottle of water and visually checking him over. "Any problems?"

"Nah," he puffed, taking a swig. "Where's Shane?"

"Leaderboard has him in fourth."

Gleeson nodded. "We're still okay then."

He rolled to a flat rock and eased himself off the bike as the next racer arrived. Chenko and Ackerman greeted him, too, and checked over the satellite information as it downloaded the racers' final times.

The man, a thin wiry fellow with dark hair, approached Kelly, a smile easing the exhaustion on his face. She matched his race number with his name. "Tim Downing?"

He nodded. "Whew. Seemed a lot harder than last year. I must be getting old."

She remembered why the name sounded familiar. She'd seen his name in the files when she'd read through them earlier. The names had been catalogued by date the applications were received. His name had been the next one after Ellen Brown, implying that they'd entered at the same time. "Did you race on Ellen Brown's team last year?"

He managed a nod. "Yeah, but we had to pull out when Ellen left. We all finished the race, but not officially." He held the cool water bottle to his sweating forehead.

"I heard she got sick."

He nodded. "Too bad. She was really enjoying the whole thing. Making lots of friends…good friends."

Something in his tone caught her attention. "What kind of friends?"

"Close friends of the male persuasion. Wish it was me, but I don't have Devin's panache. I'm just a mechanic, not a race official. Too bad for me."

Kelly wanted to ask him more questions, but her attention was distracted as Betsy Falco rolled in, a hand raised in triumph. When she turned back to Downing, he had already moved off to talk with Gleeson.

With a sigh, she approached Betsy, who seemed energized by the race she'd just endured.

"Fantastic," she crowed. "Best race ever." She pointed a finger at Gleeson and Downing. "Next event, you two will be seeing the back of me as I cross the finish line ahead of you."

Gleeson arched an eyebrow. "Competition brings out the worst in you, Betsy."

She flashed him a defiant smile. Gleeson watched her move on, and Kelly noted the contemplative look on his face.

Shane finished next and Kelly could see, even at a distance, that he had a gash on the head. Her pulse sped up as he approached.

"What happened?"

There was no cocky reply or witty joke. He pulled off his helmet. "Rock fell."

She pulled out an antiseptic wipe and pressed it to his forehead, positioned to block Gleeson and Downing's view of their conversation. "Accident?"

He shrugged. "How are you?" He caught her eye, and the intimacy of it made her look away.

"No word yet."

He let her apply a bandage to his forehead. As her fingers traced over the adhesive, she felt him relax slightly into her hands, as if his body remembered the love that had bound them together in spite of his traitorous heart. *Shane, what happened to us? To you?*

As if he could feel her thoughts, he circled her wrist with his fingers. She allowed it for one sweet moment before she pulled away and handed him a water bottle. "I need to tell you something in camp, something I heard from one of the racers."

His eyes widened with the question, but another pack of racers was entering the finish area so the discussion would have to wait. She turned to attend to the next group of people, and tried to put Shane and her own fluttering nerves out of her mind.

The evening passed in a blur, and it was nearly ten o'clock by the time all the racers had reported in. Feeling the effects of her restless night, she finally climbed into her vehicle and followed Chenko and Ackerman as they drove back to camp. She glanced at her phone for messages— again. Nothing. Uncle Bill should have been able to complete his grisly mission by now. The town where the body had been found was only six hours away, and she was sure he'd started out at first light.

Suppressing the tension building in her stomach, she focused on the events of the day. She'd found Ellen Brown's race partner, and that was surely a lead. Shane had completed the leg of the race with only a slight head wound. Was the rock fall an accident? Or had someone helped it along? She shook her head at her own thoughts. Shane's paranoia was rubbing off on her.

Still, she thought as she neared the camp, painted silver by a full October moon, where had the bicycle gone? And what did Betsy mean when she'd said Ellen was a liar? The biggest oddity of all was Ellen's disappearance. If the woman had been telling the truth, that Ackerman was with her the night of Olivia's murder, then why the need for her to lie low?

The tangle of thoughts did not distract her from the larger issue weighing on her mind. Rose. She breathed another prayer as she got out and walked to her trailer. Maybe Uncle

Bill had already called and left word with Aunt Jean. Would Kelly see it on her face the moment she walked inside?

Fear clawed at her as she stood on the porch, unable to open the door.

Shane caught up with her before she got there. "Thought you might need some company tonight."

She felt the inexplicable sting of tears. "I haven't heard, but I'm...afraid to go in."

He took her in his arms and squeezed gently, pressing his cheek to the top of her hair. "If I could do something, anything..."

The rumble of an engine startled them both. A truck pulled up, and Kelly knew with a thrill of fear who was behind the wheel. Her uncle Bill stepped out, black hair shining like an oil slick in the moonlight. He wore jeans and a tucked-in T-shirt, but he looked every inch the Tribal Ranger, even out of uniform. His dark eyes flicked over Shane before they settled on Kelly.

She wanted to run to him, but her feet were frozen in place. "Did you find out?"

He nodded slowly.

Far away, Kelly heard Aunt Jean open the door and stick her head out. She, too, seemed unable to move any farther.

"It wasn't her," he said. "Not Rose."

Kelly would have fallen if Shane hadn't reached her and hooked an arm under hers. Uncle Bill crossed the space in two long strides and circled Kelly in his arms, edging Shane away.

She tried to take some deep breaths to steady the shaking in her legs. "She's okay? Are you sure?"

"All I'm sure about is that it wasn't her."

Kelly heaved an enormous sigh as she felt her heart returning to a normal rhythm.

Uncle Bill gave her a final squeeze before he let her go. "Come inside. There are things I want to tell you."

Shane started to leave, but Kelly stopped him. "Stay, Shane. You need to tell my uncle what's going on."

She saw the uncertain look that crossed his face—wary, distrustful.

"Just lay it out and see what he thinks, that's all."

For a moment she thought he would decline, but with a shrug, he followed them into the trailer.

Shane knew Bill had gotten word of his abandonment of Kelly. He could read the hostility in the man's broad shoulders, the granite set to his tan face. He knew he deserved every bit of Bill's censure, and that Bill would likely not believe a word he said about what was going on at camp. Nonetheless, he sat with them at the table as they talked, voices low to keep from disturbing Charlie, who lay sleeping in the big bed.

Jean's face was damp from tears. She sniffled and blew her nose. "So we know our Rose is still alive."

Bill did not answer. He drummed thick fingers on the table. "No new leads, though."

Kelly straightened. "I haven't tried calling her satellite today."

"You won't get anywhere," Bill said. "Keep trying, but I don't think it'll do any good. I've tried dozens of times today. I wonder if she's left it somewhere, or lost it."

"Lost it?" Kelly gasped. "How will we find her then?"

"We'll keep looking."

Shane saw a fresh glint of tears in Kelly's eyes. "My phone was ruined. She won't know how to call me if she didn't get the text I sent."

Aunt Jean stroked her arm. "She knows my number and Bill's. We'll pass along your new number if she calls."

Kelly shook her head. "The last time I heard from her was a few weeks ago. She promised to be here for Charlie's birthday. Did either of you hear from her since then?"

They both shook their heads.

Kelly shot a look at her uncle. "What are you thinking?"

"Just got a feeling that she's in trouble, more than the drinking problem."

Kelly nodded. "I have the same feeling."

They talked for a while, the conversation eventually leading to Bill's new wife, Heather. For the first time, Shane saw Bill's face soften. "She's doing well. Taking real good care of Tina."

Kelly patted his hand. "And taking care of you, too, I see. I've never seen you look so happy."

"She wants you to come visit, with Charlie, and stay for a while."

Kelly smiled. "We'd love that. Maybe when my job here is done."

Bill cleared his throat and turned to Shane. "What is it you need to tell me?"

Shane sighed. "You all have enough on your plates. I think it would be better to keep it to myself."

Bill stared, face expressionless. "If my niece knows about it, then you haven't kept it to yourself. Let's hear it."

Shane related the entire situation to Bill, whose expression got progressively darker.

"I get that you want to support your brother, but most of the time the crime happens exactly as the cops say it did," Bill said.

Shane's jaw tightened. "I'd think after your sister's murder came to light, you might not be so sure. Cops were wrong about that, weren't they?"

Bill's eyes widened, and for a moment, Shane thought Bill might just take a swing at him. After a moment, he relaxed. "Point taken, but disproving Ackerman's alibi doesn't prove him guilty."

"All I want is to give my brother some hope. You can understand that, can't you?"

Bill's black eyes locked on his for a long moment. "I'll poke around, see if I can find out anything about Ackerman or the girl who vouched for him." He fixed a steely look on Shane. "In the meantime, don't do anything stupid."

Shane could tell Bill didn't expect much to come of it, but he appreciated help from any quarter.

Bill excused himself. "I want to get home before sunup."

"No," Kelly protested. "Stay here. It's too late to make that long drive."

Bill held firm against persuasion from both women. He kissed them both and gestured to Shane before he left the trailer. Shane followed him into the night.

Opening the door to his truck, Bill turned to Shane. "You've caused my niece a lot of heartache, son. I don't want to hear that you've caused her or Charlie any more trouble, understand?"

"Mr. Cloudman, I understand you perfectly. No one cares about Kelly more than I do."

"You got a funny way of showing it."

He couldn't argue with that. He'd shown Kelly betrayal and cowardice. "I wasn't the man I should have been."

Something crossed Bill's face, a flicker of recognition, the barest sense that he understood what Shane meant more than he would ever admit. "What matters is what kind of man you are now."

Bill gave him a long look before he got into the truck.

Shane watched him drive away until the vehicle disappeared into the darkness.

He looked toward the trailer, where the soft glow of lights outlined Kelly's profile at the kitchen table.

What kind of man are you now, Shane?

Kelly had chosen to open her arms to little Charlie. Shane had turned his back and walked away. He was the man who had let fear tear him away from everything he loved.

What kind of man was he now? A fool. A fool who could never undo the wreckage of his life.

He looked up at the moon, now cloaked in clouds, just as the rain began to fall.

Was I so bad? he found himself wondering. *Was I so bad that You had to strip everything away from me when I was thirteen?*

What had happened that day so long ago continued to haunt him, to follow him through every moment of his life. It was at the root of what he'd done to Kelly, and perhaps why he'd managed to involve her in his life once again. Everything had gone wrong in that moment, cemented in that one colossal failure when he let his brother drown.

Bill's words echoed back to him. *What kind of man are you?*

The rain poured down now, snaking cold trails down his back and across his face. Maybe he'd never really become a man at all, and he would forever remain that tortured thirteen-year-old kid.

"Shane?"

He felt Kelly's hand on his arm, but he did not turn to face her.

"Why are you standing out here in the rain? Come inside. I want to tell you what I found out at the race today."

He turned then. Her face, lit by moonlight, beads of water collecting in her hair, was so beautiful it knifed through him. "Just forget it. Your uncle was right—I was wrong to involve you."

Her hand tightened. "Maybe, but I didn't give you much

choice. What's done is done and now I have something that might help you."

"But you shouldn't be helping me," he snapped, his voice strained. "It's not right, Kelly. I don't deserve your help—not after what I did."

The silvery light caught the frown on her face. Her voice was so low he almost missed it.

"Shane, why did you leave me?"

He wanted to answer her with a kiss, to let her feel the grief that flowed through his veins and held him prisoner, and taste the love that lay underneath, the love for her that had never waned. Silence stretched between them, broken only by the patter of the rain. "Because I'm a fool," he whispered.

She looked away for the barest of seconds, and when she turned her face back to his, the vulnerability was hidden under the determined mask. "I told you that many times," she said, and they both laughed.

She'd returned them back to a safe place where they could connect superficially, and he was grateful.

She pulled him toward the scant covering offered by the porch and shared what she had learned from Tim Downing. "Ellen left abruptly. There's something strange about that. She didn't say goodbye to anyone or even take a reasonable amount of time to recover from being so sick. If Tim was her teammate…"

In spite of the leaden feeling still lingering in his stomach, Shane felt his hopes rise. "Then maybe he still has contact with her. An old phone number or something."

"Exactly what I was thinking."

"Thanks, Kell." He left the porch.

"You're welcome. Where are you going?"

"To talk to Tim." He thrust a thumb at a trailer on the far end of the row. "His light's still on."

Kelly fell in step next to him. "Let's go then, Sherlock."

He smiled. "I'd rather be Watson. Sherlock wore that goofy hat." In a few moments they knocked on Tim's door. He opened it, clad in sweatpants and a T-shirt, a motocross magazine in his hand.

"Hey, what are you doing here at this hour?"

"Sorry to intrude," Shane said. "Can we talk to you for a minute?"

Tim nodded and invited them into the tiny trailer. An ice pack lay on the kitchen counter. Tim grinned sheepishly. "Couldn't sleep. My back didn't much like that uphill track today."

Shane nodded, feeling his own muscles silently complaining. "I hear you. Listen, we won't take up much of your time. Kelly said you were on Ellen Brown's race team last year."

He nodded. "Sure, until she left."

"I've been hoping to talk to her," Shane said.

Tim frowned. "Why?"

"I wanted to ask her a question about something that happened." Shane held his breath, waiting to see if the explanation would be enough for Tim.

He laughed. "Man, that girl sure didn't have any trouble attracting men."

Kelly nodded. "She and Devin Ackerman were an item."

"Yeah, they were pretty into each other. I always thought that was weird."

"What was?"

"That after she got sick and left, Devin never seemed to know where she went. The team wanted to send her flowers or something, but he couldn't tell us where. Didn't seem to want to even talk about her at all."

"Did you ever contact her?"

Tim looked sheepish. "Yeah. I figured maybe after the

race we could get together for coffee if she was really over Devin, that is, but we just talked. She made it clear she wanted to put everything about that race behind her."

Shane tried not to appear too eager. "So you talked to her? A phone call?"

"Yeah."

"Would you happen to still have that number?"

He wrinkled his brow. "I might have it back home in my files. I could call there tomorrow after my roommate gets back from work and ask him to check."

"That would be great," Shane said.

Tim jutted his chin at the window. "Looks like we might have some discretionary time if the storm kicks up. Can't do the canoe and run if the weather is miserable."

Kelly and Shane stepped out on the porch.

"Tim," Kelly said. "One more thing. When Ellen got sick, where did they take her for treatment?"

"Pine Grove Clinic. It was the closest place to our camp."

They thanked him again as they left.

Shane walked so fast, Kelly had to trot to keep up. "If he can get me a number, this might be the break I need."

"I hope so."

He walked her to her trailer and waited while she climbed the step. As she opened the screen door she pulled her satellite phone from her pocket.

Her face white, she turned to Shane. "I got a message."

"Who's it from?"

"Stormy," Kelly whispered.

Shane couldn't figure out the significance, but something in Kelly's posture told him the message was about to change things. "Stormy?"

Kelly clutched the phone in her hand. "Stormy is my sister's nickname."

TEN

Kelly's legs trembled as she led the way back inside. "My mother always called her that because she was moody as a teenager. You never knew which way the wind was blowing with Rose." Kelly shook her head. "I don't recognize the number."

"It doesn't make any sense." She dialed quickly, her stomach clenching into tighter and tighter knots with every ring. No answer.

She texted quickly. *Rose, where are you? We're worried.* Though she stared at the tiny screen, no reply text appeared.

She played the message again for them all to hear, first checking to be sure Charlie was sleeping.

"Hey, sis. It's me, Stormy. I'm gonna get back for the birthday, I promise. Going to call back as soon as I can and get the details about your new job and where we can meet. It's…I hope I'm doing the right thing. I'm really trying." There was a swift intake of breath. "I gotta go. Kiss you know who for me and tell him I love him."

Kelly looked puzzled. "You know who? It's like she's talking in code or something."

Aunt Jean and Shane advised Kelly to call her uncle. She did so, reaching him on his satellite. He told her he would have someone run the phone number and get back to her.

"Don't do anything until I have more information," he warned before hanging up.

Kelly sighed as she clicked off the phone. "He doesn't want me to call until he checks it out. But what if she's in trouble? What if she needs my help?"

Shane held up a hand. "Your uncle is right. There's something strange about this situation."

Kelly agreed. "There's a reason she wasn't using her real name, and it's odd that she didn't call me on her satellite."

"Maybe she lost it, as your uncle said," Shane suggested.

"Could be. She's been unable to pay for the phone and had to rely on borrowed phones before, but something in her voice worries me."

Though they played over possible scenarios for a half hour more, they came no closer to any conclusions.

"Best thing is to do nothing for now," Shane said.

Aunt Jean nodded. "We don't need any more trouble around here." She checked her watch. "Oh my. It's after midnight. Weather report says there's a whopper of a storm coming in." She shot Shane a look. "Even so, you should be getting some rest in case your race isn't cancelled, don't you think?"

He laughed. "Yes, ma'am. I'm off to bed then."

Kelly walked him to the door. "So much has happened today. I woke up worrying that my sister was dead, and now I've got a message from her. Why wouldn't she use her own name? Why Stormy?"

He shook his head. "I'm not sure, but I do know you should do what your uncle advised."

"This from a man who always insists rules are just suggestions."

He dropped a kiss on her cheek, lips warm and soft. "Good night, Kell."

She felt the tingle where his lips touched her skin. He

shouldn't be in her life anymore. She'd cut those bonds and moved on. She was a stand-in mother now with a career and a future to think about. So why did his touch seem to leave an indelible mark on her?

With a sigh, she went to look in on Charlie. He slept soundly in spite of the winds that picked up speed throughout the night. She listened to the branches scraping along the top of the trailer and passed the hours worrying constantly about her sister.

At six o'clock in the morning she was sipping coffee, checking her phone every few minutes to see if another message had come in. It hadn't, but the storm outside had picked up, with howling winds and curtains of rain muddying the campground.

She saw Shane, head ducked under the rain, heading for the lodge at 7:30. Charlie appeared at her elbow and climbed into her lap. "Hungry?" she said, kissing the top of his head.

He nodded. "Can we go eat with the racers?"

Kelly glanced at Aunt Jean, curled up in her bed at the far end of the trailer. "Okay. We'll go get breakfast and bring some back for Aunt Jean."

She bundled him in a jacket and pulled on a windbreaker before they splashed madly through the puddles and into the lodge. They arrived laughing and breathless. Martin Chenko grinned at them. "Well, there you go. Two people who aren't letting the weather get them down." He knelt next to Charlie and pulled a black baseball cap from his back pocket, then settled it onto the boy's head.

"Now you've got your Desert Quest cap. You're an official racer."

Charlie beamed. "Can I ride in a canoe?"

Chenko considered. "I'm sure we can get you a canoe trip as soon as the weather clears. How about that?"

Charlie smiled, and Kelly added her thanks. "It's going

to be a boring day inside for him, but you really made his morning."

Chenko nodded. "Pretty soon he'll be big enough to race along with the grown-ups." Chenko sighed. "They grow so fast." He waved a hand around the rapidly filling lodge. "I feel as if these fifty folks are my children, in a way, but I guess my real baby is this race. That's why I get so wound up when things go off course."

Devin approached and handed Kelly a cup of coffee. "No worries. By this afternoon, I have no doubt the weather will be cleared up. We'll be back on track tomorrow."

"Did you find the missing bike yet?" Kelly asked.

Devin's face tightened for a moment. Then his smile was back in place. He squeezed Kelly's shoulder and leaned close. "Now don't tell me you're buying into Shane's conspiracy theory." He whispered in Kelly's ear, "The guy has slipped a gear or something."

Chenko raised an eyebrow. "Still, I want the bike found."

"We'll find it," Devin said. "As my mom always says, 'The solution is there even if you don't want to see it sometimes.'"

Kelly smiled. "Sounds like a smart lady."

"Oh, yeah. She's a doctor, and Dad's a software engineer. I've got great genes."

Chenko raised an eyebrow. "You should be in college then. Parents would pay, wouldn't they?"

"Hey, I did my time in college—two years at UCLA."

"And you dropped out? Left a prestigious school for this?" Chenko asked.

Devin snorted. "You sound just like them. They think I should get a real job."

Chenko sighed. "If someone hands you a chance to make something of yourself, I can't understand why you'd throw that away."

A flicker of anger crossed Ackerman's face. "I just made myself into something different, that's all. Following a new path doesn't mean it's the wrong one." He shrugged and turned back to Kelly. "Anyway, maybe we can get together sometime today and go over the plans for tomorrow," he said with a glance at the sky. "It's got to stop raining sometime."

Betsy joined them, curling her arm through Devin's and pulling him toward her for a kiss. She beamed a smile at Kelly. "Bad news about the weather, huh?"

She smiled back. It seemed that the tiff between Devin and Betsy had blown over. She was glad to have Devin's attention directed somewhere else. Chenko moved away and Shane joined Kelly, disappointment on his face.

"Looks like Downing won't hear from his roommate until evening. Race event is definitely called off for today." He sighed. "I feel like a caged tiger."

Charlie trotted up. "See my hat? I'm a real racer."

Shane dropped to his knee and fingered the cap. "That is a great hat."

"Gonna go on a boat ride later," Charlie said.

Shane's face clouded. "You are? That's neat."

Kelly watched them chat. When Charlie climbed up at the table to eat, he called to Shane. "Sit here."

Shane shot an uncomfortable look at Kelly. She shrugged. Certainly Charlie was going to get tired of just herself and Aunt Jean for company. It wouldn't do any harm to let him spend some time with Shane. The child began unloading the two dozen coffee stirrers he'd stashed in his pockets. Shane laughed and showed Charlie how to play a rudimentary game of pickup sticks.

Kelly remembered the phone call she needed to make and walked away a few paces, keeping the two in her line of sight. She dialed her former classmate's number and got an answering machine. "Hey, Julia, it's Kelly Cloudman." She kept the small talk short and got right down to her question. "Your clinic treated a patient named Ellen Brown last year in October. I wondered if I could ask you something about your recollections. Give me a call back when you can."

Her phone vibrated as she was putting it away. It was Uncle Bill.

"Kelly, I got the info back on that number."

"Great." Kelly's breath caught. "Tell me."

"It's a pay-phone number."

"A pay phone? Where?"

"Town called Ash Ridge, about two hours north of your location."

Her mouth dropped open. "So close? Rose could be two hours from here?" Her spirit soared. "I'm going to call. Maybe she's waiting there. She needs transportation or something. I've got to tell her how to find me."

"Hold on," Bill said. "I've talked to the police there. They are going to keep an eye out for Rose, and they'll call me if they spot her. I've sent a photo."

"So they can make sure she's okay then. They'll…"

He cut her off. "Kelly, they're just doing me a favor. Rose is an adult, and she hasn't broken any laws that we're aware of. As I said, they are helping me only out of courtesy."

"I should go there. Find out if anyone has seen her."

"Leave that to me. I'll drive up and ask around as soon as I can free up some time."

But that might be too late if she's in trouble.

The silence lengthened. "Kelly, do not go to Ash Ridge by yourself, do you understand?"

She sighed. "Yes."

"I mean it. We don't know what's going on. Could be dangerous."

"I know, but it's killing me. I can't even text her now.

What happened to her phone?" She knew her uncle had no answer, only the same feeling in his gut that she had in hers.

The feeling that Rose was in trouble.

Shane enjoyed watching Charlie's chubby fingers trying to gently retrieve the coffee stirrers. He was so intent on his task, he didn't notice anything around him. Lonnie had been like that, able to zone in so completely on digging a hole or building with blocks that the world around him disappeared. The pain seared through Shane again.

Charlie isn't Lonnie, he told himself. He's not going to get hurt because of you.

Shane looked up to see Kelly pocketing her phone, a grave look on her face as she joined them. "Uncle Bill traced the number back to a pay phone in Ash Ridge."

Shane whistled. "Practically in the neighborhood."

Kelly nodded and sat heavily. "The police are keeping an eye out for her, but not officially." He could sense her mind reeling, sorting through the possibilities. "He doesn't think I should go look for her."

Shane sighed. "He's probably right. If…" He shot a glance at Charlie. "If Stormy is in some kind of trouble, you won't make things better by jumping in the middle of it."

Kelly's eyes narrowed. "You sound just like my uncle."

"I'll take that as a compliment."

She drank a sip of coffee and then beamed those dark eyes straight at him. "But what would you do?"

"What do you mean?" he asked, though he knew exactly what she meant.

"If it was your brother. What would you do?"

Shane glanced around the crowded lodge, filled with disappointed racers discussing the weather. "Oh, I think you know what I'd do."

She smiled. "I think you're right."

In another hour, after the breakfast things were cleared away and race plans were tentatively rescheduled for Friday, weather permitting, Shane found himself helping Charlie into the backseat of his Jeep. Kelly's car was still in the shop awaiting repairs, but at least Charlie's car seat had dried out.

She wondered aloud if it was safe to take Charlie along, but she'd decided that going to a town with lots of people and Shane by her side would pose no immediate danger. Besides, she'd said she wanted Charlie with her. When they were apart, it felt as if a piece of her was missing.

They made their departure as casual as possible, so as not to elicit any questions. Kelly retrieved the medical backpack from her race vehicle, tucking it on the floor near her feet.

"Habit," she said.

The only resistance they'd gotten was from Aunt Jean as she sat stroking the aged cat.

"Your uncle doesn't want you to go," she reminded them.

Kelly kissed her. "We'll be back soon, I promise."

"And what do I tell Bill if he calls, looking for you?"

"Tell him the truth. I don't think he'll be too surprised," Kelly said with a laugh. "He always said his nieces would make his hair turn gray."

As he pulled out onto the highway, Shane could imagine what Uncle Bill would say to him, but there was no way he would let Kelly drive to Ash Ridge by herself, especially if she was right and Rose really was in trouble. Part of him chalked her up behavior to difficult circumstances and the devastating effects of addiction, but Kelly had entertained his belief in his brother, and he would do the same thing for her sister.

It was one way, maybe the only way, he could stand by her after what he'd done. The rain continued to pour down on them as they drove. Kelly's phone rang and she snatched it up.

"Hello, Julia." She covered the phone and mouthed to Shane. "It's my friend who works at the clinic." She listened intently, peppering the caller with questions until she disconnected. "She remembers when Ellen Brown was brought in."

Shane waited for her to put her thoughts in order.

"Julia said the doctor first thought it was an overdose. Blurred vision, delirium, dilated pupils."

He frowned. "Drugs? Unusual for an endurance racer. They tend to err on the health-nut side."

She nodded. "But tests confirmed it was some sort of toxin. They treated her with a purgative and a mild sedative. She demanded to be released as soon as she came through the worst of it. Refused any further testing. Julia said she practically ran out the clinic doors as soon as they unhooked her IV."

"Why the hurry?"

"Good question." Kelly looked out the window at the patches of grass undulating against the pull of wind and rain.

"What does your friend think?"

"She told me the rest strictly off the record. The doctor was an old-timer, and he remembered a case he'd had as a young man. A couple of teens showed the same symptoms, only their condition worsened into convulsions and they both died. The final conclusion was that the kids had made tea from a toxic plant."

"What kind of plant?"

"Jimsonweed."

Shane's breath caught. "The kind that grows wild all over South Dakota."

She nodded. "It's all poisonous, from the leaves to the seeds."

"Tim said Ellen was a tea drinker."

"Uh-huh. It wouldn't have taken much to add a little something to her beverage."

Shane drummed his fingers on the steering wheel. "So someone poisoned her? Maybe Ackerman did it, to convince Ellen she'd better stick by her story and not undermine his alibi."

"And she was too afraid to go to the cops? I'm not sure what to think." Kelly lapsed into silence until Charlie began to wiggle, and she started up the "Old MacDonald" song.

Shane found himself joining in, in spite of himself. He added as many funny lines as he could think of until all three of them were laughing. Shane caught a glimpse of Charlie's face in the rearview mirror, lit from the inside with laughter. His eyes sparkled just like Kelly's, and for a moment it nearly overwhelmed him.

He gripped the wheel until he felt Kelly's fingers on his wrist, bringing him back to the here and now.

"It's the turn," she said, giving him an odd look. "Left here."

They drove into the town of Ash Ridge, population 1275, according to the sign that welcomed them. Charlie was happy to get out of the car when Shane pulled into the parking lot of a small strip mall. The mall boasted a gift shop, a weight loss clinic, an ice cream store and a dental office. Across the street was an old but well-kept hotel called the Desert Inn.

Kelly looked up and down after she let Charlie loose under the covered walkway. "I'm not sure what to do first."

Uncertainty was unlike her. He realized how hard it must

be for Kelly, keeping life normal and happy for Charlie while she worried relentlessly that something had happened to his mother.

And she kept it together all by herself.

Not today, Shane vowed. *Today you're going to help Kelly and Charlie.* "Let's try the hotel. Maybe she planned to stay the night."

They walked through the drizzle into the hotel. Charlie went immediately to the rack of tourist pamphlets and perused them as if they held the key to the universe. Shane approached the young man at the front desk, who greeted them with a friendly smile, his shock of red hair startling on his pale face.

"Looking for a room, sir?"

Shane's cheeks warmed. "No. We're just looking for this lady's sister. We're having some trouble locating her and wondered if she checked in here."

His smile dimmed. "I see. Well, actually I can't tell you things like that. It's confidential."

Shane nodded. "I understand, but she may be in some trouble and we need to find her."

He shook his head. "No, sir. I'm sorry. I suggest you contact the sheriff."

"Please," Shane said, but the boy pressed his lips together.

"Sorry, sir. I'm not going to lose my job for you."

With a sigh, Shane led them back outside.

Kelly looked so discouraged and tired as they started toward the street that he picked up Charlie. To his surprise, Charlie snuggled close, his arms around Shane's neck. He gave the boy a tentative squeeze and Charlie seemed perfectly content to lay his head on Shane's broad shoulder, as if they had known each other forever.

As he caught the stricken look on Kelly's face, he knew

she was surprised, too. She reached up to take him and Shane let her, feeling keenly the loss of the boy's small arms around his neck. She didn't say a word, but he read it all in her eyes.

I'm not letting him get attached to you. You left us. And you'd leave again if I let you back in.

He wished he could say it wasn't true, that another chance with Kelly would make a new man of him, but in his heart he did not believe it.

Bill's words rang through his memory: "What kind of man are you now?"

Kelly already knew what kind—the kind who let her down.

He looked away, staring at the street, watching but not really seeing the cars roll by.

"Excuse me," a soft voice said.

They both turned to find a young girl with hair caught in a tight ponytail looking at them.

"Yes?" Kelly said.

"I work at the Desert Inn. I heard you talking to the manager." The girl looked closely at Kelly. "You look a lot like your sister."

ELEVEN

Kelly was so surprised she gasped out loud. "My sister? You saw her? She was at the hotel?"

The girl nodded. "I have a sister, too, and I worry about her all the time since she ran away." Her gaze faltered. "I know what it's like."

"Please," Kelly said. "Please tell me what you know about my sister."

"She checked in yesterday morning. Didn't have any luggage, and she paid ahead in cash. She told me she stayed in Ash Ridge for a while four years ago and the people had been nice to her. She asked me if Sheriff Rickers was still in charge at the police station."

"She lived here?" Kelly was unsure what question to ask next.

Shane frowned. "Was she going to the police?"

The girl shrugged. "I don't know. I saw her heading to the gift shop about an hour after she checked in. Then all of a sudden she was back, checking out, without even having spent one night here. The manager asked her if everything was okay, and she said yes but her plans had changed. She looked upset. Scared even."

Kelly felt a surge of frustration. "Where did she go? Do

you know how she left town? The bus? A cab? Did she have her own car?"

"I'm sorry," the girl said with a sigh. "That's all I know. I've got to get back. I could get in trouble for telling you that much."

Kelly reached out a hand and touched the girl's shoulder. "Thank you."

They both watched her walk away. Kelly didn't know whether she should cry or rejoice. Rose had been there just a day ago. She scanned the length of the main road. It was a quiet community with nothing to hint at what had spooked her sister. She felt Shane's hand on her back, urging her to cross the road.

She allowed herself to be guided along, too confused to make any decisions of her own.

On the other side, they passed a church with a small sign in the window that read Angel Heart: Help is here. Shane stopped so abruptly she almost plowed into him from behind. "What?"

"Angel Heart. For some reason that name rings a bell." Though he frowned at it for a while, he couldn't figure out why the name struck a chord.

Kelly was impatient to go forward. "Let's start at the gift shop. They can't have very many employees. Someone will remember her."

Holding Charlie firmly by the hand, Kelly pushed into the Gifts a Million store. The shelves were crowded with knickknacks, porcelain figurines and candles. It might not have had a million items, but it had enough to make her dizzy. She wondered how they kept an accurate inventory with such a hodgepodge of goods.

Charlie spotted the shelf of boxed toy cars. He dropped to his knees to examine the selection. Kelly smiled. She pictured Rose in here, combing through the same collection, looking for the perfect birthday gift for Charlie. Nearly four-year-old Charlie, the child she hadn't seen since she'd left him with Kelly. Kelly had assumed that Rose's unreliability was solely the result of her drinking and drug abuse, but now she was beginning to think there was some other force at work, keeping her on the run.

Lord, help me find her this time. Please.

"Charlie," Kelly said. "Your birthday is on Monday, and I haven't gotten your present yet. Which one of these would you like?"

Charlie's eyes widened, considering his choices. He picked a package of ten cars in fiery reds and yellows. "This one."

She took it to the counter to pay. The clerk was an older lady with papery white cheeks. She peered over the counter at Charlie. "What a big man you are. Did I hear something about a birthday?"

Charlie grinned. "Mama Kelly's gonna get me these cars."

"Well, Mama Kelly is certainly nice to you, isn't she?"

As she rang up the sale, Kelly asked about Rose. "She came in yesterday, in the morning probably. She might have bought some toys, cars even."

The lady scrunched up her face in thought. "Oh, yes. I do remember a young lady about your age, and come to think of it, she looked a lot like you. And you're right. She did buy a toy dump truck, I think."

Kelly's heart sped up. "She's my sister."

"Does she live around here? I just bought this place last year so I'm afraid I don't know everyone yet."

"She was just passing through. When she left, did she mention where she was going? Did you see where she went?"

"No, honey. I'm sorry. She didn't say much. She seemed

friendly at first, but then something seemed to change. She just bought her toy and left."

Kelly slumped. "Thanks, anyway."

Shane wrapped an arm around her shoulder as she turned away. "It's okay. We know more than we did an hour ago."

She nodded, blinking back a sudden onslaught of tears. So close. She noticed a little battered chair and table and a selection of dog-eared books put out to distract little shoppers. Charlie slid into the chair and held out a book about fire engines. "Please read?"

Kelly crouched next to him and read the story, all the while her thoughts racing ahead. Should they go to the police and ask about Rose? Call Uncle Bill and let him know what they'd found out? They still had no real proof that anything sinister had happened to Rose, but the terrible feeling of dread continued to build inside Kelly.

Shane was just finishing up purchasing a small item, which he slipped into his pocket. He stopped suddenly. "Kell…"

She followed his finger, which pointed to a glossy paper tacked to the wall behind the register. Drawing closer, she saw it was a flyer for Desert Quest. There was a series of pictures of faces she'd come to know well—Devin, Chenko, Betsy and dozens of racers.

Shane's blue eyes bored into hers. "Do you suppose," he said, "that your sister saw this?"

"She probably did, but why would it upset her?"

Shane's voice seemed to come from far away. "I don't know. Your sister's situation can't be connected to the race. That would just be too coincidental."

Would it? Kelly's mind whirled. When Charlie was done with the story, they walked outside. The ice cream store beckoned, wafting sweet fragrances onto the chilly street.

Inside, they chose a battered table in the corner. Charlie and Shane licked their cones, but Kelly was too agitated to eat.

Her sister had told the hotel clerk she'd been to Ash Ridge before, for long enough to be somewhat familiar with the town. Kelly hadn't ever been in contact with her sister with enough consistency to know where she was staying. What was going on?

When Charlie hopped down from the table to fetch a napkin, Kelly whispered to Shane, "Four years ago Rose would have been pregnant with Charlie."

Shane nodded slowly. "If she lived here, she must have stayed with somebody, or rented a place." He looked at her. "None of my business, but who was the father? Was she with him then?"

Kelly shrugged. "I don't think so. She was in a bad relationship, someone she wanted to get away from. Could be that's why she came to Ash Ridge in the first place."

"Pretty tough situation, pregnant and alone."

Kelly didn't add, *And struggling to stay clean and sober.* "I wonder why she wanted to see the sheriff."

"There's only one way to find out," Shane said, slam-dunking his rolled-up napkin.

"Do you think he'll tell us anything?"

Shane smiled at her. "How could he refuse my charm?"

She laughed in spite of herself. "All right, Mr. Charming. Let's go."

The sheriff was away at a training. His deputy, a long lean man with bags under his eyes, greeted them at the front desk. "Anything I can help you with?"

Shane watched as Kelly explained their search for her sister and showed him a picture her uncle forwarded to her borrowed phone.

"We think she lived here before, and we wondered if the sheriff knew her."

He squinched up his eyes in thought. "I've only been here for four years now, but I don't remember a gal named Rose."

"She might be using the name Stormy."

His eyebrows arched. "What kind of trouble is she in exactly?"

"We're not sure." Kelly bit her lip.

Shane wanted to put a hand out to support her, but he ignored the urge. "Can you leave a message for the sheriff to call when he gets back in town?"

The officer nodded and gave Kelly a sympathetic look. "This town is close to the highway, so we get people in and out on a regular basis. Hard to know everyone."

She thanked him, picked up Charlie and they left.

Back on the street, Kelly let out a sigh. "I guess there's nothing else to do then but go back to camp and wait for the sheriff to call."

Shane nodded, his eyes drawn to the church and the Angel Heart sign. Why did the name strike a chord with him? He considered suggesting they check it out, but Kelly looked so downcast he changed his mind. Besides, Charlie was beginning to droop in her arms.

They made it back to the car. Shane glanced up as he opened the door for Kelly. A white car sped by, the driver's face in shadow. He caught only a glimpse, an impression really, of the driver.

"Kelly, get in quickly."

She froze for a moment before belting Charlie into the car seat and sliding into the passenger seat. "What is it?"

He didn't answer, quickly backing out and heading in the direction the car had taken, away from town. For several blocks he didn't see any sign of the white car until they passed a side street where it was idling. He continued on to the next turn and doubled back. The driver must have anticipated his maneuver because he was now heading in the other direction, toward the traffic light where they had crossed the street earlier.

"Who is it?" Kelly demanded.

"Not sure, but he definitely doesn't want us to catch up, does he?"

The car headed toward the green light. Shane pushed a little faster. The light was turning yellow, and the white car slowed.

"See if you can get the license plate number," he called to Kelly.

A van pulled in front of them. "I can't see it," she hissed in frustration.

The driver of the van honked at the white car, nearly stopped now at the yellow light. As soon as it turned red, the white car took off, leaving the van honking angrily.

For a split second Shane thought about peeling around the van and running the light, but Charlie was in the back of the car. He could never risk endangering the child, or Kelly, for that matter. Grinding his teeth in frustration, he slammed a hand on the steering wheel.

"Who was that?" Kelly asked, a trace of fear in her voice.

"I'm not positive. I only got a glimpse of his face."

"Who do you think it was?"

Shane turned to her. "I only saw him for a second, but I think it was Gleeson."

Her mouth dropped open. "Gleeson? Why would he be here?"

"More to the point, why would he be following us?"

"I thought he was just your race partner."

Shane replayed his prior encounters with Gleeson in his mind. Recalling one, he said, "I saw him out at night.

Seemed like he was searching for something, but he wouldn't come clean about it."

"What would he be searching for?"

"I don't know. I got the feeling from the beginning that he wasn't just here for the race. He asked a lot of questions, he wondered…" Shane felt his cheeks warm. "He asked if you and I were a couple."

"Why would he care about that?"

"Not sure." Shane's suspicions flared into overdrive. "But he was the one who came to the clinic where you worked, right? Devin brought him?"

She nodded slowly. "Yes, I treated him for a sprain."

"Could he have faked it?"

"Why would he?"

"Maybe Ackerman wanted him to."

She shook her head. "But that makes no sense. Why would Devin have him fake an injury? How would that possibly benefit him?"

"It provided an introduction, a means to hire you as race nurse."

Now she glanced at him. "What in the world does that have to do with anything?"

It was his turn to shake his head. "I'm not sure, but I'm beginning to think Rose might know the answer."

She closed her eyes. "This is all spinning out of control. My sister never even met Devin, as far as I know."

"But you don't know a lot about your sister. You didn't know she stayed in Ash Ridge until just a few hours ago."

Kelly's face crumpled, and he felt like kicking himself for adding to her pain.

"You're right," she whispered. "Right now I feel as if I don't know anything about my sister. How could my twin be such a stranger to me? Maybe I didn't try hard enough. I was angry when she left."

He took her hand, accelerating as the light turned green, not surprised to find that the white car had vanished. "This isn't your fault. I'm sorry for making it sound that way. We'll figure out how this all fits together—I promise."

She raised her damp eyes to his. "But you can't promise we'll find my sister."

He wished with all his heart and soul that he could.

She closed her eyes, and he wondered if she was praying. He tried to think of what to say, how to ask God to help Kelly. But God had turned away from Shane, left him in a dark shadow from which he could not escape. There was no help there, and no comfort.

He grabbed the wheel with both hands and squeezed. *Find a way to help her.* His heart added the rest. *And then find a way to let her go.*

She shivered, and he turned on the heater.

Charlie sighed. "I want to go play with Paddy Paws. How much longer?"

Shane remembered his purchase at the Gifts a Million store. He pulled a toy motorcycle from his pocket and handed it over the backseat. "Here you go. An early birthday present from me. Something to play with while we drive back to camp."

Kelly shot him a grateful look. "That was nice of you."

He shrugged. Nothing he ever did would make up for turning away from the boy, but he found himself enjoying being around Charlie, in spite of the memories of Lonnie that tugged at his heart. He checked the time. "Just after one. We should be back in a couple hours. My brother is due to call and I want to ask him a question."

She didn't answer. At first he thought she was lost in thought. A few seconds later he picked up on her rigid posture, the fingers clutching her seatbelt. He looked over and saw unadulterated fear on her face.

"What?" he asked.

She could not speak at first. "Pull over, Shane. Right now."

He let a few cars pass and eased over to the sidewalk, alarm circling his gut. "What's wrong?"

She pointed to the backpack at her feet. He saw nothing unusual.

Then a flicker of movement caught his eye. A corner of the backpack was unzipped, a cord trailing from it. When the cord began to uncoil itself, the truth snapped into place.

With a look of utter terror on her face, Kelly watched the snake slither from the backpack and curl around her ankle.

TWELVE

Kelly felt the weight of the creature looping around her ankle. The sky was still clouded and she dared not bend over to look at the thing. As it was she was fighting to keep from screaming and leaping out the car door. She remembered the day her uncle had been bitten by a prairie rattlesnake.

Run, Kelly. Run and get Aunt Jean.

By the time she'd returned, his ankle was swollen to twice its size and Uncle Bill was pale and sweating, lips trembling. They'd gotten him to the clinic in time for the antivenom to take effect, but Kelly had never forgotten that fear. For several months afterward, she'd been afraid to walk outside alone.

Her ears were ringing. Was it the dry, raspy sound of the rattles?

Another terrifying thought assailed her. Would the reptile get into the backseat? Charlie's much smaller frame would be no match for the hemotoxins in the snake's venom. Shane was saying something in a low, soothing tone, but she was too scared to hear. His door eased open and he got out. Panic swelled inside her. Shane was leaving her, just as he had before. She wanted to scream, to bang her hands against the window and beg him to stay, but she remained stone still in her terror.

"Mama Kelly?" Charlie asked sleepily from the backseat. "Where is Mr. Shane going?"

"I don't know, Charlie," she managed.

He unbuckled his seat belt.

"Stay in your seat, honey." Her voice wobbled. He must not come close to the snake, which was now nosing its cold head under the cuff of her jeans.

Please, God. Please don't let Charlie get bitten.

Charlie stuck his head over the front seat. "Are we going to stay here?"

"We'll go in a minute. Play with your motorcycle for just a little bit longer." Her fingers curled around the door handle. The only escape was to jump out, hope it didn't bite her and open the back door for Charlie to get out. Her eyes blurred from a sudden onslaught of tears.

On the count of three, she told herself.

She only got to two.

The door eased open without her help and Shane was there, eyes wide and intent. He shone a small penlight down into the dark space around her feet. Slowly he reached out a hand.

"No," she breathed. "It will strike you. Just get Charlie out. Get Charlie out," she hissed as loudly as she dared.

Shane continued to shine the light on the snake, which felt cold and tight around her leg. Her legs trembled and she wondered if the snake sensed her fear, like the terror of some small animal about to be devoured.

When she thought she could no longer contain a scream, Shane's hand darted out toward the snake.

Kelly shrieked in spite of herself. Shane backed up, holding the snake behind the neck, its length dangling clear to the ground. Charlie popped over the front seat again. "A snake! Is it gonna bite you?"

Shane smiled at him. "No. I've got him behind the head here so he can't bite. It's a bull snake—it's not poisonous, anyway. I'm going to go put him over there in the bushes. Do you want to come and see it crawl away, Charlie?"

"Yeah," Charlie crooned. He followed at a safe distance behind Shane. Kelly watched Shane kneel and release the snake, Charlie's small hand on his big shoulder. After a moment, they returned to the car.

Charlie stopped to collect some shiny pebbles from the ground. Kelly got out and leaned against the car, shivering. Shane pulled her into his arms and ran his hands up and down her back. Kelly could not hold in the sobs now, try as she might. "I thought you'd left."

He stiffened and squeezed her tighter. "No. I was right here the whole time. It's over now."

Her tears dampened his shirt, and she gave herself over to the relief until Charlie put his arm around her leg. "Why are you crying? Did the snake bite you?"

She brushed her sleeve over her eyes and knelt next to him. "No, honey. I was just…surprised. I'm okay."

He nodded. "That was a long snake. It crawled away, didn't it, Mr. Shane?" There was a hint of fear in the boy's eyes.

Shane patted his head. "Oh, yes. That snake crawled right away to find his family. He's probably got a little son who's almost four, too."

That brought a smile to Charlie's face. "How do you know all about snakes?"

"My brothers and I used to go on snake hunts all the time."

"Brothers?" Kelly asked. "I thought Todd was your only brother."

Shane looked away, bending to pick up a stick and breaking it into bits. "My younger brother died."

Something in those words made her think Shane had experienced a whole lifetime that she wasn't aware of.

"Anyway, we should get back and put in a call to your uncle. He'll be mad, but he needs to know what we found out."

Try as she might, Kelly couldn't make herself get back into the car.

Shane, noticing her hesitation, took out the backpack and carefully unloaded its contents, checking every pocket and crevice. Then he packed it up and did the same with the car, looking under the seats and in the glove box. "It's fine. No more hitchhikers."

She rebuckled Charlie in the back and climbed in, tucking her feet up on the seat. They drove in silence for several miles before Shane voiced the question that was tumbling over and over in her mind. "When did someone put a snake in your backpack?"

She wanted to say it was just an accident, that the snake had climbed into the pack at some point on its own, but she knew that wasn't possible. Someone had put it in there, and the car heater had awakened the reptile. "I used the pack as the racers crossed the finish line yesterday. Then I put it in the car until I grabbed it this morning."

"Was the car locked?"

"Yes."

He frowned. "So that means anyone on the race staff could have gotten access. They have a spare set of keys in the office, I'm sure. That means Ackerman, Chenko or anyone who spends time with them could have sneaked the keys and put the snake in your pack. Or it could have been done while we were here in town."

Her stomach tightened. "Gleeson?"

"I wouldn't put it past him. It's possible he jimmied the car open himself. Wouldn't surprise me."

"But why?" She folded her arms tightly around herself, to hold the current of emotion in. "There's no benefit to scaring me. What would Gleeson gain by doing that?"

Shane shook his head. "I'm not sure. It's possible he's working for someone else."

"That still doesn't answer the question. If Devin is responsible for Olivia's death and he knows you suspect him, he'd be after you, not me."

Shane shifted on the seat. "Unless he knows you're important to me."

His words were so low, she almost didn't catch them. "What?"

"Maybe Devin knows you're important to me, and threatening you will distract me."

"Am I?" Her voice came out almost a whisper. "Am I important to you?"

He looked at her. "You'll always be the most important woman in my life."

She was speechless for a moment. The most important woman? The woman he had walked away from without a backward glance? She locked eyes with him for a moment, and there was such sadness there, all her anger ebbed away.

He kept his eyes on the road. "Kell, I think you should get out of here."

"You think I should leave because I'm in danger?"

"That's exactly what I think, and now you have proof that it's not my imagination. That snake didn't crawl into your backpack by itself."

"But I'm so close to my sister. If I leave now, I may never know what happened to her."

"The police will investigate."

"She's an adult with alcohol problems. She hasn't committed a crime. They won't investigate too hard."

"Your uncle will."

"He'll try, but he's a Tribal Ranger with no authority here. Plus, he's got a new wife and a foster child at the moment."

He took her hand and pressed it to his face, tracing his lips over her palm.

Her pulse quickened and she cupped his cheek, feeling the warmth of his breath on her skin. The touch made her dizzy and her mind ran wild, back to the moment at the car when she thought he'd left her again.

It became clear in that moment, as clear as the wide open sky above them, washed clean by the torrential rains. He was right; she had to go—but not for the reasons Shane believed.

She had to leave because there was a raw place deep inside her that clung to him, hungered for his touch and would never be fully healed. Every day spent with him only deepened her longing for the man who had left her long ago.

Blinking hard, Kelly pulled her hand away. She would not, could not allow her soul to be ripped asunder again. "You're right. I'll make arrangements to leave right after the race tomorrow."

The rest of the trip passed in slow-motion silence. Mile after mile unfurled before them as they headed back to town. He should have felt relieved that Kelly had decided to do the smart thing and leave. He should have felt a great weight lifted off his shoulders, but instead, the weight seemed to have settled on his heart.

It's the right thing, Shane. You made your choice. Kelly isn't yours.

The truth tore at him, embedding a sliver of pain deep down in his heart that would not let up.

Back in camp, he stayed with her as she called Uncle Bill and explained their findings. As Shane predicted, Bill did not take the news of their trip well. His voice on the speakerphone was clipped and angry.

"I'll check it out, and you two stay out of it."

Kelly told him about her decision to leave the next day, and he sounded slightly mollified. "Good. Come and stay with us here in Rockvale until you find a position." He even managed a chuckle. "It will be good to have Charlie here for his birthday, and Rose will know where to find us."

Shane excused himself when his own phone buzzed. He stepped outside, the cool evening air a balm on his face.

"How are you, little brother?" Todd sounded tired and distant. "I promised I would call, but this is the last time— no sense in it."

Shane ignored the worry that rose anew in his gut. "I'm making progress here."

No answer.

"Todd, I need to ask you something. Why do I know the name of an organization called Angel Heart?"

"Angel Heart? I haven't heard that name for years. It's a Christian group that helps unwed mothers."

"How do you know about it?"

"Before we got married, Olivia helped out at an Angel Heart. She told me she really loved the work, but something bad happened and she quit and moved here. That's when I met her."

It made sense. Shane remembered seeing a pamphlet at Todd's house about the Angel Heart organization in a box of Olivia's things that he'd found on a shelf after the police had left. Shane's instincts prickled. "What happened?"

"Olivia didn't like to talk about it."

"You need to tell me, Todd."

"Why? What has this got to do with the present? That was years ago."

"Tell me," he repeated grimly.

"Olivia worked with a group of unwed mothers, getting them jobs, feeding and housing them at the local churches, if necessary. She used to ask for food donations from local restaurants and stuff like that. One time she went to a diner, near Ash Ridge I think it was, and she witnessed a crime of some sort. She told the police and all that, but nothing came of it. Mostly she wanted to put it behind her and never think about it again. She wouldn't even tell me about it because it upset her so badly."

"Did she ever talk about a woman named Rose Cloudman?"

"Cloudman? Is that your girlfriend's sister?"

Not my girlfriend anymore, he thought grimly. "Yes."

"Hey, I've gotta go, Shane. Time's nearly up."

"Todd, did she ever mention Rose Cloudman?"

"No. She never spoke about the women she helped. As I said, she wanted to erase whatever happened back then. I have to go."

"Call me later."

"I'm not calling again, Shane."

"Don't say that."

"My lawyer said the trial is scheduled to start the end of the month. He's not optimistic."

"I'm working on it. I'm getting closer to an answer."

"There is no answer, Shane. I'm going to prison for killing my wife."

"No, you're not."

"Get on with your life, little brother, and forget about mine."

The disconnect sounded loud in Shane's ear. Desperation rose inside him, along with the strong feeling that Olivia and Rose were connected somehow. He felt more and more convinced that Rose had been one of Olivia's wards at Angel Heart, and whatever crime she had witnessed somehow held the keys to what had happened to both women.

He headed back to his trailer. He should be winding down, getting his body in shape for the canoeing and running section of the race in the morning, but he knew he could not sleep until he powered up his laptop and did a little poking around.

As he unlocked the door, Gleeson appeared out of the shadows. "Hey, Matthews. Where you been?"

Shane turned to face him. "You know exactly where I've been because you were following me."

Gleeson's eyes rounded in innocence. "Me? You must have me confused with some other guy."

"I don't think so." He moved closer. "Why don't you tell me what you're after?"

Gleeson's smile vanished. "Why don't you? As long as we're airing our dirty laundry here, maybe you should go first. Your last name isn't Matthews; it's Mason. You're a horse rancher who signed onto this race to dig up some dirt on someone, and I have a strong hunch that someone is Devin Ackerman."

It was almost a relief to Shane to have it out in the open. "Why does it matter to you what I'm after if you're just here to race?"

"I'm a jack-of-all-trades. Been in the military, been an insurance investigator. Sometimes I do some off-the-books security work."

"For Ackerman?"

He shrugged. "For whoever pays me. I run license plate numbers on all the racers as a precaution. Took about two seconds to find out who you really are."

"And what are you supposed to do about it?"

"I just make sure things run smoothly."

"By getting rid of me? Did you do a number on my bike?"

"Hey, you're my race partner, remember? I really am in this thing to win. The security job is on the side."

"So you worked on the race last year?"

"Maybe."

"But things didn't run so smoothly then, did they?" Shane felt his pulse pound. "One of your race cronies killed Olivia Mason, my sister-in-law."

"And you're here to clear your brother by finding out the truth? Listen, kid, I admire your loyalty, but this is just a race. There's no one hiding from the law here, as much as you want there to be. It's hard for you to face the truth about your brother."

"My brother didn't kill her."

"As I said, you've got admirable loyalty."

"If you were here last year, you remember Ellen Brown. She left suddenly after giving Ackerman an alibi."

His eyes narrowed. "So?"

"So what happened to her? She took sick and then vanished. Didn't even want to stay in the hospital."

"You've done some research."

"Seems to me she was afraid. Maybe Ackerman threatened to hurt her if she told the truth."

"You're tilting at windmills."

"Ackerman would like me to think so."

Gleeson sighed. "Look, kid. Why don't we just concentrate on the race. Ackerman's an adrenalin junkie—same as we are—that's all. He has nothing to hide."

Something in his eyes made Shane press further. "But someone does. That night you were out in the woods. You were looking for something." His mind put it together. "My bike. You were looking for my bike, because you think someone really did sabotage it."

Gleeson glanced away.

Shane laughed grimly. "So we do have something in common. You believe someone here is trying to keep me from figuring out the truth, don't you? Otherwise you wouldn't have been out looking for my bike."

"I'm saying no such thing. It pays to be cautious." He turned to go. "You and your girlfriend should remember that."

Shane was on him in a minute, grabbing his arm and spinning him around. Gleeson's hands came up reflexively in a fighting stance. Shane gripped him tightly. "What are you saying about Kelly? Is she in danger? Did you put that snake in her backpack to scare her?"

"Snake?" There was a glint in Gleeson's eyes before he pulled away. "No. I can't stand snakes. That was someone else's little trick. I'm just telling you that people who go around digging up trouble usually find it, and those around them pay the price."

"Is that a threat?"

"No, just an observation." He left, walking away from the pool of porch light and melting into the shadows.

THIRTEEN

Uncle Bill's angry voice rang in Kelly's ears as she finished the bowl of spicy chili Aunt Jean had made. Even the hot food did not dispel the memory of the cold snake coiled around her ankle.

"He's just mad because he worries," she said. "And he is probably frustrated that he didn't know Rose stayed in Ash Ridge."

"I know."

"So close and she might as well have been a million miles away. Oh, I forgot," she said, heaving herself out of the chair and putting Paddy Paws down on the floor. "I was out for my walk when the rain let up and I ran into one of the racers, a Tim something or other." She pulled a scrap of paper from her purse. "He left you a phone number of a mutual friend, I think he said."

Kelly grabbed the scrap eagerly. Tim's handwriting was terrible, but she could make out the name Ellen Brown and a phone number. This might be the break Shane had been waiting for since his brother was arrested. "I need to go give this to Shane. Will you be okay here for a little bit?"

"Of course." She hesitated. "Honey, I know it's not my place, but Shane hurt you pretty bad last time."

Kelly's face flushed. "It's not what it looks like. We're

just working together on a project. I'm…I'm actually going to leave the race after the next event."

"Why?"

She shrugged. "Plenty of reasons."

"Are you sure one of them isn't because you're starting to have feelings for Shane again?"

Again? Her cascade of feelings for Shane had never ebbed. The overwhelming crush of love, followed by a pain so profound she did not think she would survive it. Aunt Jean took her hands, and she saw deep compassion in that wrinkled face.

"Don't misunderstand me," she said quietly. "Forgiveness is the very sweetest thing, Kelly, and if you can find it in your heart to forgive Shane, then that will bless you both. Just be careful, honey, that you don't ask more of him than he can give."

She squeezed Aunt Jean's hands before gently pulling hers away. "I learned that lesson already. I'm not asking him for anything." She dropped a kiss on her aunt's cheek and hastened out the door.

The light in Shane's trailer outlined him sitting at the table, staring at his laptop. She knocked and he opened it, a startled expression on his face. "Everything okay?"

"Yes." She held out the scrap. "It's from Tim. It's Ellen's number." The hopefulness that flickered across his face for a moment took her breath away.

He snatched up his satellite phone and gestured for her to sit next to him at the table as he dialed. "I hope it's not too late to call." He tensed as he set the phone between them.

A woman's voice answered. "Hello?"

"Is this Ellen Brown?" Shane asked.

"Who wants to know?"

"My name is Shane Mason. I'm participating in the

Desert Quest Race. I know you raced last year, and I wondered if I could ask you a question."

Her tone was icy. "I don't know what you're talking about."

"Last year, you raced with Tim Downing. You got sick and had to leave."

Silence.

"You provided an alibi for Devin Ackerman in the killing of a woman by the name of Olivia Mason here in South Dakota a few days before the race began."

More silence.

"Please, Ellen. I'm not trying to hurt you or make trouble. I just want to go over the details of your statement."

"Are you a cop?"

"No."

"Then I have nothing to say to you."

Shane leaned toward the phone. "I'm not accusing you of anything. My brother is in jail for the crime, and he didn't do it. I'm trying to help figure out what really happened."

"I'm sorry about your brother, but I'm not talking anymore. That was the worst time in my life, and I just want to forget about it."

"Just…"

"No. I'm not exposing myself to a psychopath ever again. Don't call me anymore because I'm changing my number."

The dial tone sounded loud in the quiet room. Shane threw himself back in the chair with an exasperated groan.

"A psychopath?" Kelly mused aloud. "Was she talking about Devin?"

"Ackerman, Chenko—even Gleeson could be involved for all I know." Shane got up and stalked around the small space. "I feel as if I'm going in circles."

Kelly nodded. "Every time we discover something, it upsets the balance of what we already believed." She looked at the open laptop and saw what he'd typed in the search box. "Angel Heart?"

He nodded, settling into the chair again. "My brother said Olivia was involved in the organization. It's a group to assist unwed mothers."

Kelly started. "And Olivia worked in Ash Ridge? Did she know my sister?"

He sighed. "Todd said she never talked about it. She witnessed a crime four years ago, before they met, and it really traumatized her. That's what I was about to dive into."

Kelly moved close to watch the screen, ignoring the feeling of his muscled shoulder against her cheek and the faint scent of his musky aftershave. He began to type terms in the search box; Ash Ridge, the year and murder. It took only moments to get a hit. Shane squinted at the screen. "It's an article about a murder, a local waitress at Buckthorn Diner just outside Ash Ridge almost four years ago." Shane tensed. "Here it is. It says the killer was spotted by a woman named Olivia Tantino as he fled. The killer escaped."

There was a grainy picture of a group outside the crime scene. A waitress clutched an apron to her mouth. Several police officers and bystanders were assembled outside the diner.

Kelly's mind whirled. "It's not a coincidence. It can't be. My sister was in Ash Ridge four years ago, and she was pregnant. Your sister-in-law was there, too. Do you think they were somehow both connected to the murder of that poor waitress?"

Shane's eyes darted in thought. "The more we learn, the more it seems as if their lives are somehow intertwined. Could be the person who killed that waitress also killed Olivia because she could ID him."

Kelly peered at the picture. Could her sister have even been there in the crowd? But why had she left Ash Ridge, pregnant and alone? Something about the picture niggled at her, but she couldn't figure out what.

She felt bone-weary. Dropping her head on her arms, she sighed.

"None of it makes sense," she groaned. "My sister, Olivia. A murder four years ago. Your bike, the snake—how is it all connected?"

Shane rested his hands on her shoulders and gave her a gentle massage. "Maybe it's not. Could be we're trying to tie things together that just don't fit."

His fingers continued to squeeze, and she relaxed in spite of herself.

"But it's a good thing you're going home, just in case."

She sat up, a trickle of fear washing through her. "But if you're right, and someone here killed Olivia, that person is going to come after you."

He smiled, that roguish grin that still made her weak in the knees. "I'm tougher than I look."

She put a hand on his cheek. "No jokes. Not now. You could get hurt, Shane. Or killed."

"As long as you and Charlie are safe, that's the important thing."

She was suddenly pulled against his chest, his arms circling her body in a warm embrace. "I don't want you to get hurt," she whispered, feeling the pulse of his heart. "You should leave, too."

"I've got to see this thing through to the end." He brushed her hair away from her face. "I've got to."

She was lost in a cloud of emotion, in the feeling of his arms around her. There it was again, the shimmer of grief in his voice when he spoke of Todd, as if he knew from experience the agony of losing a brother.

"Shane, when you were talking to Charlie, you told him

you used to hunt for snakes with your brothers. Was your other brother younger?"

He jerked backward as if she'd struck him. "Yes. He drowned."

"How?"

He turned away. "I don't talk about that."

"Why not? When we were together before, we shared everything."

He closed his eyes for a moment, and when he opened them his face was cold and distant. "Some things aren't meant to be shared."

She took a step back, repelled by the hardness in his tone. All that time, she'd told him everything—about Rose, about her mother, about her fears and triumphs. All that time, he'd been keeping something from her, something that rocked him to the core.

"Those are the things that usually need sharing most of all," she said quietly as she moved to the door and left.

The first thing Kelly did the next morning was go straight to the lodge, where she knew she would find Devin and Martin Chenko busily planning the day. She was not disappointed. They sat at a far table, heads bowed over a computer screen. A few racers were up. Betsy and Gwen sipped coffee at a quiet table. Gwen waved at Kelly as she came in, and Betsy raised her coffee mug in greeting. Kelly waved back but did not veer from her uncomfortable mission.

It was unprofessional to leave a job midstream, but after the snake incident and Charlie's brief disappearance, she was beginning to worry about his safety, too. And there was something about the way Gwen looked at Charlie that unnerved her.

You're lying to yourself, Kelly.

The reason she was leaving—the real reason—was the way her heart quickened whenever she saw Shane looking at her, and the way being in his arms made her feel. She could never again risk becoming lost in those feelings. Squaring her shoulders, she approached the two men.

Chenko looked up . "Good morning, Kelly. Join us."

Devin stood and pulled out a chair for her. "Going to be a great day."

She nodded. "I've got some bad news. I need to leave after this leg is over."

Chenko's brows drew together. "Leave? You can't leave; we've got another event after this."

"I'm sorry. I know it's not the best scenario."

"Not the best? It's going to put us in crisis mode." Chenko held up his hands. "Please don't back out on your commitment here. If it's a matter of money…"

"No, no, it's nothing like that. I've contacted a few colleagues of mine who are available to replace me."

Devin leaned toward her. "What's behind this decision? Has someone treated you badly here?"

"No, nothing like that. It's a family issue."

Her stomach constricted, and she found herself babbling. "It's Charlie. I'm not sure this is a good place for him. It was my mistake committing us to the race."

"Charlie's doing okay here, isn't he? Plenty of room to run and your aunt to stay with him. What better place for a kid?" Chenko asked.

"Come on," Devin said. "Give us another chance. We can help you. Get a babysitter from town if your aunt isn't up to it." He came next to her and put his arm around her shoulder.

"I really don't think it will work out," Kelly said, taking a step away.

Chenko sighed. "Please, Kelly. This race is my whole life

right now, and I don't want anything to derail it. At least think about it, and we can talk again tonight. Will you do that for me?"

She saw the fatigue on his face. It was wrong to leave him in the lurch. "All right. We can talk again tonight."

Kelly returned to her trailer and found Aunt Jean hanging up the phone. Her face was grave. "What's wrong?"

"It was Uncle Bill. He tracked down the chief of Ash Ridge who went through the files on the death of that waitress."

"And?"

"And the sheriff confirmed that Olivia saw the killer as he ran. She provided a vague description to the police."

Kelly nodded. "Yes, we know all that. Shane suspects it might have something to do with why she was killed."

Aunt Jean pursed her lips. "She wasn't alone."

"What?"

"Olivia reported that there was a woman with her, a woman she was helping through Angel Heart. The woman refused to go to the police. She took off, and Olivia didn't know where to contact her."

Kelly's heart thudded to a stop. "What was the woman's name?"

Aunt Jean took a deep breath. "Olivia never knew the woman's real name, but she went by the name of Stormy."

Shane grabbed a quick breakfast and helped load the canoes before they headed to the river. He didn't see Kelly or Charlie. More than anything, he wanted to get the race over with and send Kelly on her way.

He felt raw inside, her question the previous night had opened up the gaping hole in his heart again. Would things have been different if he'd told her about Lonnie? No. She would have known much sooner that he was not the man she thought he was.

What kind of man are you now?

He gritted his teeth, determined to finish the next leg of the race and send Kelly home safely. Then he could get to the bottom of things. Maybe he could hire a detective to track down Ellen Brown. He'd tried to call back but, true to her word, Ellen's phone was disconnected. Or he could pump Gleeson for more information. The man was closemouthed, but he also was beginning to suspect someone—his boss, maybe—was up to something. It had to be related to the crime Olivia had witnessed in Ash Ridge years before.

He had no more time to contemplate as they made their way to the river's edge. The race was intended to be a frantic trip through class-four rapids, followed by a fifteen-mile run at the other end. Racers would spend the mandatory six-hour rest period at an overnight checkpoint before starting the last leg, the ropes course and spelunking event, in the wee hours of Sunday morning. Awards would be given out on Monday.

Then it would be over.

A dull throb started in his chest. It felt as if it was over the moment he'd convinced Kelly to leave.

Get your head in the race and help your brother.

The river water rushed violently along as the racers made their way down to the water's edge. Kelly caught him by the arm as he clipped on his helmet.

"My sister was with Olivia at the diner," she whispered in his ear. "She saw the killer too, but she took off rather than go to the police."

He gasped. "So they really are connected."

She nodded. "My uncle is meeting with the sheriff in

person today to go over the files. He's going to join us when we drive back."

Shane swallowed. She'd be taken care of, safely back in her uncle's custody.

Suddenly Kelly lurched forward into him. He grabbed her to keep her from falling.

"Sorry," Betsy said, hefting her canoe. "I'm a better driver in the water."

Gwen followed along, her eyes darting from Kelly then away toward the river.

Shane helped Kelly regain her balance, letting go in spite of his overwhelming desire to crush her to his chest and bury his face in her long hair.

She gave him a tentative smile. "Thanks."

"You got it."

She didn't have to say the rest—it shone clearly in her brown eyes.

"Yes," he said, giving her a wink. "I'll be careful. Don't want you to have to work too hard today."

He joined the line of racers fanned out at the edge of the roaring water. The rain, combined with the extra water released from the nearby dam north of them in preparation for storm season, made the flow a daunting sight. Truth be told, Shane didn't much like the water. His skill at canoeing came because he'd forced himself to learn, thrusting himself into the element that God used to take away his brother.

He felt the stubborn flare of anger rise up inside him. *I'm going to beat this river today.*

He hefted the canoe by the crossfork, thumping the sturdy Royalex sides as he moved into position. The vessel was not a traditional calm-water canoe. It was a small C-1 craft, more like a kayak than a canoe, meant to be easily maneuverable. The athlete knelt in the front and employed a one-bladed paddle. Gleeson would be in the first group to start, along with Betsy, Tim and the others. Shane would be toward the middle, with Gwen behind him. He cast a look in her direction. She looked terrified.

"You okay?" he called above the sound of the water.

She nodded, her eyes still fixed on the ferocious current.

He pointed to a spot a half mile down. "Could get tricky down there."

She flashed a wan smile. "That's what Betsy said."

They watched the racers in front of them get into their canoes and take off with whoops of excitement.

Shane fastened his personal flotation device and tightened the strap on his helmet. His safety equipment was all accounted for—throw rope, knife, carabiners clipped in their locked position. Stomach tightening, he saw Ackerman approach with a starting gun in his hand.

The sight burned itself into his mind. Had he held a similar gun when he murdered Olivia and framed Todd for killing her? Their eyes locked, and Devin flashed him a cocky grin. "Water's rough. Can you handle it, Matthews?"

"I'm not afraid of rough water."

Devin's smile vanished. "We'll see if you still think so at the finish line, provided you get there."

"I'll get there, don't worry."

"I won't," Devin said.

Your mistake. Shane steadied the canoe in the eddy and knelt in the seat, looping the thigh straps securely. Gripping the paddle firmly, he tensed for the starting gun. Out of the corner of his eye, he saw Gwen do the same.

Somewhere up on the bank, he knew Kelly was watching.

FOURTEEN

At the sound of the starting gun Shane flipped a neat eddy turn, and in a moment, he was caught up in the rush of the tumbling waves. Though he wore a paddle jacket and pants, the cold of the water splashing over the gunnels momentarily left him breathless as the torrent carried him away at a dizzying speed.

He'd scoped out the course ahead of time and knew the first danger to overcome was the sieve, about a half mile downriver. The sieve funneled the water between an enormous boulder and another lower shelf of rock. He'd been in the river enough to know that the water compressed between the two rock barriers was under higher pressure than the water around it, so turbulence would be a factor. It would test his white-water skills to the limit. He wondered briefly if Ackerman and Chenko really understood how dangerous a swollen river could be.

He could not hear any sounds from the other racers, just the roar and slap of the river as it shoved him along. Keeping his shoulders loose and using the paddle to weave himself into the frantic flow, he made his way along, adrenaline pumping through his system. As the sieve approached, he pushed against the foot pedals, making sure his legs were securely rammed into the thigh straps. One careless move and he could easily be flipped upside down. Though he'd managed an Eskimo Roll to right himself before in calmer waters, the violence of the current and the prevalence of the rocks that knocked occasionally into the bottom of his boat made him reluctant to try it. This was not a polite river, and calm-water techniques were not going to work in this race.

The rocks loomed before him, and for a moment he felt a twinge of panic as his speed increased. The bank flashed by as he hurtled faster and faster. He wondered, just for a split second, if the river would beat him today.

Not today. Not ever again.

Gritting his teeth, he gripped the paddle more securely and forced his torso to relax, to move with the water instead of fighting it. The sieve loomed ahead; he could feel the change in the water under his bow. Like a bullet from a gun, his tiny craft rushed toward the narrow opening between the rocks. Paddling alternately on both sides to keep the boat from being swamped, he held his breath as he approached the gap. A wave he had not accounted for took him by surprise, and his canoe cracked into a rock with a thunk, but did not tip. In a moment, he was through, triumph surging in his gut.

He'd beaten the river, at least for the moment. His canoe bobbed and weaved as he continued along. An instinct pricked at him to turn around. He shot a quick look behind him. He couldn't see much past the curtain of rock and water. The ominous feeling flared brighter in his gut.

Though speed should have been the first thing on his mind, he propelled himself into the slow-moving eddy at the extreme edge of the water. He looked back across the river as several racers made their way by, their faces creased in concentration as they approached the sieve and exultation as they slipped through it—some without any trouble, some with a good deal of buffeting against the rocks. He searched for any sign of Gwen, wondering how she had fallen so far behind. The look on her face at the starting line had revealed a level of fear that could be dangerous around white water.

Finally he spotted her approaching the river bend, black hair frizzing out from beneath her helmet. He was not close enough to see the look on her face, but her body was rigid, paddle slapping into the water as she fought to control her boat.

He held his paddle to one side, giving her the signal that the route he'd taken would see her safely through. She did not copy the signal, so he was not sure if she'd even seen him. As she drew closer, he could see more clearly that she was fighting the water.

He knew that was a disaster in the making. Fear makes you the loser.

He knew. He remembered.

The memory of the rocks scratching his fingers as he frantically clawed underwater, searching for Lonnie. The moment of stark terror when he stood, waist deep, too scared even to scream. The cold water enveloping him as his brother tumbled into the fast-moving creek, snatched away in a flash. A thirteen-year-old, taking his brother out to play in the creek.

"Water's high, Shane," Lonnie had said on that bright fall morning.

"Not too high for me. We can go back if you want."

Lonnie had answered with that look of hero worship on his face. "Not too high for me either."

One minute, Shane was showing off for his brother, and the next, frantically pounding through the water, trying to save him from being washed downstream.

He wondered if Lonnie had been scared, as scared as Gwen obviously was now, before he drowned.

Shane did not understand why God had punished him that day, and every day since. Pain and unadulterated rage seeped to the surface again.

What was it about Shane Mason that made him unlovable in God's eyes? A soul to be crushed at age thirteen, reduced to fighting the tide that seemed determined to snatch everything away from him. Lonnie, Todd…

And Kelly.

His eyes automatically sought the bank, trying to pinpoint where she might be. Maybe today would be the last time he would ever see her. She would move on and leave him behind. Never again would he see her looking at him with that mix of love and exasperation.

Water roared in his ears and stung his eyes.

By now, his group of racers had all passed, shooting down the next five miles of river. Only he and Gwen remained.

Gleeson would be nearly finished, starting on the next leg of the race. Shane should be moving on, too, yet he remained in the eddy, watching Gwen's harrowing approach toward the sieve.

Get moving. You're here to keep in the race. Stay in it or you can't help your brother.

But he did not go. He remained tucked into the eddy, mesmerized by Gwen's approach. She was abreast of the sieve now, the change in the water flow jerking and twisting her canoe.

Don't fight too hard.
Feel the water and work with it.
Don't let the fear make you helpless.

Gwen plunged her paddle into the water, causing her boat to turn sharply in the other direction. The force of the water pinned her against the rock, and for a moment she was caught there, her face frozen white and stark against the gray rock. Then she began paddling frantically until she lost her grip and the paddle was ripped from her hand. The water rushed in over the gunnels.

Shane saw her panic, read it in the motion of her flailing hands as she tried to free herself from the thigh straps.

"Gwen!" he shouted, over the roar.

She did not hear him, trapped in her own terror as she battled with the torrent.

Water poured over the gunnels, filling the interior. As it pooled around her waist, she stopped fighting and lifted her face to the sky.

The canoe turned over, taking Gwen with it.

Kelly stood on the rise above the river, watching the action unfold beneath her. Her heart lurched as she saw Shane approach the narrow gap of rock, easing only slightly when he'd made it through. She did not understand why he'd pulled into the eddy and stopped. He did not wave his paddle vertically in the air, indicating there was an emergency.

She got out her binoculars and trained them down on the water. His attention was fixed on the racer behind him. She had to scan her clipboard to learn that it was Gwen Falco. Though Kelly had never tried canoeing, even in still water, she could see that Gwen was struggling. As soon as her canoe smashed against the rocks, Kelly was galvanized into action. She grabbed her bag and scrambled down the twisting trail toward the water, shouting into her radio as she went.

"We have a racer in trouble. I need help."

Though she, too, wore a GPS unit, she knew that by the time anyone got to their position, it would be too late. Chenko was already miles downstream at the finish line, and Devin was stationed a mile upriver to start the last group of racers. She prayed he'd gotten the message in time to stop them from entering the water.

Slipping on loose debris, she half fell, half ran to the water's edge, taking a moment to get her bearings. Then she saw the two rocks projecting from the water several yards ahead. She hoped Gwen had been able to right herself or get out of the boat. Maybe she was clinging to the rock, waiting for rescue. The angry roar of water punching downstream next to her made her doubt the woman would have the strength.

She turned the corner just as Shane started to push out of the calm eddy water back into the current.

"Shane!" she yelled before he completed the turn.

He stopped, grabbed a packet from his canoe and tossed it to her.

"Tie it onto something," he yelled.

With trembling fingers she grabbed the throw rope, unfurling it and tying it as securely as she could around the nearest boulder and tossing him the other end. He grabbed it and paddled out of the eddy, ferrying across the crush of the current.

The radio crackled. "Kelly? I'm on my way. What's the status?" Devin shouted.

She could not answer, her mouth suddenly dry as she watched Shane's progress.

Somehow he managed to force his canoe across the angry river, looping back around behind the rocks before he turned and allowed his boat to rejoin the current, following the path that Gwen had taken.

Her breath froze in her chest as Shane's canoe rushed up to the rocks where Gwen was still upside down. He was going too fast; he would lose control and be crushed against the rocks.

Devin's voice came across the radio again, louder this time.

"What is going on there?" he demanded.

"Shane!" she screamed as his boat slammed into the rock with an ominous crack. The white water obscured her view for a moment and then, to her horror, she saw Shane's canoe careening down stream.

Empty.

Shane knew it was sheer lunacy to hit the rock intentionally, but he could think of no other way to get to Gwen Falco before she drowned.

When the side of his canoe hit the rock, the force shook through his body and left him momentarily stunned. Only the slight movement of his boat as it threatened to skid off the rock and reenter the current brought him to his senses. With hands stiff from the cold, he undid his thigh straps and shoved away the craft, which went spinning crazily out into the current.

He knew he had to get to Gwen quickly, or there would be no chance for her survival. He made a loop from the throw rope and tossed it over the top of the rock, which imprisoned Gwen's craft. His aim was off, and the rope was sucked away into the turbulence.

Teeth gritted, he managed to grab the end and pull in the length of rope. This time, his throw was perfect and the loop caught around the pinnacle. He pulled it tight so it now stretched across the river, from the place where Kelly had tied it to the spot where he was going to attempt a rescue. He began to haul himself from his precarious perch over to Gwen. The thundering water struck at him with such explosive force, he felt as though he was being battered by a thousand angry fists as he crossed the narrow gap between the two rocks. Hand over hand, he made his way along, bones vibrating from the impact.

Just as he thought he could not maintain his grip on the

rope any longer, he made it to the other rock where Gwen's canoe lay overturned. Letting the water work with him now, pinning him as it had Gwen's canoe, he bent down and, still holding the rock with one hand, grabbed the gunnel and tried to heave the boat over.

It didn't budge.

With a rising sense of panic, he let go of his own hold and yanked on the gunnel again, this time with both hands. The boat flipped only halfway, but it was enough.

He grabbed Gwen's shoulder and pulled her close to his body, again using the force of the water to hold them steady against the rock. He was not sure if she was alive or dead, her body limp in his, head drooped down over his clasped arms.

She couldn't be dead.

"Gwen!" he yelled. He felt a slight movement from her, but he could not tell if it was a sign that she was conscious or the result of the rushing water moving her body. It didn't matter. He was going to get her to shore, to help.

Holding her to him with one arm, he risked opening the Velcro pouch on the back of his personal flotation device and released the tow tether, clipping it with the carabiner to the rope that Kelly had secured. Then he grabbed another short length of rope he had snatched before letting his own boat go, and used it to tie Gwen's body to his own. Now their lives were entwined. They would drown together or survive, if he was strong enough to get them to shore.

He didn't say a prayer as he positioned himself on his back, Gwen in his arms. He knew God had no love for him, but maybe He had a spot of compassion for the woman whose life Shane held in his hands. Doubts assailed him like the stinging drops of water that stabbed at his eyes.

You'll let her down. She'll die. She'll drown. It will be another death on your conscience.

"No," he said aloud. He shook off the negative thoughts and eased out into the water on his back. The current took them immediately, pulling them away from the fixed rope until the tow line snapped taut with a breathtaking jerk. He fought the urge to get his legs under him.

Standing was the deadliest thing you could do in white water, with cracks and crevices waiting to trap an ankle or foot under a crush of water that would easily push victims facedown in a heartbeat. Struggling to keep his feet pointed downstream and arch his back, he allowed the current to pull them into the center of the river. After a moment to rest his muscles, which were now screaming in protest, he began the painful process of pulling them up via the tow line until he could grab the fixed rope. Rocks banged into his back and his legs as he fought against both the current and Gwen's dead weight.

The cold water numbed him, making his fingers clumsy. An incredible weight seemed to be pulling at him, sucking him down into failure, urging him to give up. He caught sight of Kelly up on the bank, her hands at her mouth.

Kelly...

He fixed on her there, and though his vision was obscured by the foam that battered his face, he concentrated on memories of her dark hair, the brown eyes that danced with delight as she watched little Charlie play—the devotion he'd seen there before the hurt, the faith that nestled deep down in spite of the losses she'd sustained.

Hand over hand he battled, flashes of his surroundings assailing his senses: the ice-cold pull of the water. Kelly waiting on the shore. The seemingly endless length of rope extending before him. Fingers clawing for purchase, the wet rope sliding out of his grip.

His whole body was growing numb, Gwen's weight drawing him deeper into the raging water. His hand slipped off the line and he hung there for a moment, desperately trying to keep his hold. But he and Gwen were once again yanked to the end of the tow rope. This time, he knew, he did not have enough strength left to get them back.

Despair filled his mind as he struggled to keep on his back, to hold Gwen's head above water for as long as he could.

Then he felt a tug, and slow movement against the current.

He opened his eyes to see Devin Ackerman there, attached to the fixed rope by his own tether, hauling them both back. His face was tight with the effort. He yelled something that Shane could not make out.

Another few minutes and they were close to the bank. Kelly splashed in to assist them as Devin unstrapped Gwen and Kelly half supported, half dragged Gwen from the water.

Devin turned his attention to Shane next. Gripping Shane's PFD firmly in one hand, he undid the quick release on the tow tether and began to haul him toward shore.

The events unfolded in a watery haze. Did Ackerman stumble? Did a sudden vicious jerk of water unsettle him?

Or had Ackerman finally found the perfect way to end Shane's investigations?

Shane did not have a moment to decide as he found himself tumbling free, back into the angry current.

FIFTEEN

Kelly struggled to carry Gwen away from the water. She checked for a pulse, relieved to find one fluttering under the cold skin. She pulled an emergency blanket from her pack and wrapped Gwen up as best as she could.

Gwen moaned, and her eyelids twitched. She opened them briefly. "I'm…"

"Quiet, now," Kelly said, patting her hands. "You're okay. Just rest. Shane got you out of the water so you're going to be okay."

Devin ran up, and his look made her bolt to her feet. "What? Where is Shane?"

He shook his head, hands splayed open in a gesture of helplessness. "The current took him right out of my grip."

"What do you mean? Where is he?" She darted to the water's edge and found no sign of Shane.

Her nerves propelled her forward, but Devin grabbed her arm. "Where are you going?"

"Stay with Gwen. I'm going to find him."

"No, you'll drown. The water is ferocious. I'll radio ahead. Chenko will send someone."

"That will be too late," she hissed, ripping her arm away from Devin's hold.

Gwen was sitting up now, looking from Kelly to Devin in dazed horror. "I'm so sorry, Rose."

Kelly froze, staring into Gwen's face. "What did you just call me?"

Gwen started to cry. Kelly's need to know pierced her insides, but even more pressing was her overwhelming fear for Shane. Without another moment's hesitation, she took off, doubling back to the trail that rose above the bank.

From there she would be able to spot him.

Her legs felt like lead as she ran upslope, pushing aside the branches that slapped at her face. Climbing until her lungs burned, she stopped to scan the river. Down below, the water took a sharp turn, thundering over rocks and scouring the steep banks. She saw no sign of him in the roiling water. She needed a higher vantage point so she sprinted again as fast as she could on the uneven ground. Finally, at the top of the low cliff she stopped again, her eyes poring over every wave, every rock, straining for any sign of Shane in the tumult below.

A flash of color caught her eye—Shane's helmet. He was lying in a shallow eddy. Heart hammering, she ran back down the trail until she found the nearest area that was passable. Sitting on the ground, she skidded and plunged down the rocky slope, kicking aside foliage, jumping over stone outcroppings until she hurtled onto the bank. She scanned the river edge until she found him again, his body splayed out in the shallow water, very still.

Fear soaked into every pore as she ran to him.

God, please, please, please. Though she could not say the words, she knew God already saw the terror in her heart, the all-consuming fear that Shane was gone. She made it to his side, relieved to see that he had settled on his back, the PFD keeping his head above the shallow water that cradled him.

"Shane," she whispered, her eyes scanning for blood, fingers fumbling for a pulse at his neck. "Can you hear me?"

He was still, his face deathly pale except for the bruise along one cheekbone. She reached under his arms and pulled him away from the water, onto drier ground. Still he did not move. Her fingers shook so badly, she could not tell if the pulsing was the shaking of her fingers or the beat of his heart.

She placed her fingers on his wrist, trying to find the comforting rhythm there, when suddenly his fingers circled hers. She looked up to find his blue eyes looking at her, fogged with pain.

"Lonnie. Did you find him? Did you get him out?" he whispered.

"Shane." She stroked his cheeks with her palms. "Oh, Shane, you're alive."

"Lonnie? Did you find him?"

She tried to quiet him. "You're confused. You got swept away."

"Lonnie's gone?" His voice was so small, like a little boy's.

"Honey, your brother Lonnie is dead. It was a long time ago," she said as gently as she could.

He blinked, and the fog lifted from his eyes as he struggled to sit up. He turned his face to the thundering river behind him, and she watched as the memory of what had happened returned. "It wasn't Lonnie. It was Gwen," he said.

"Yes. She's okay. You saved her."

His shoulders sagged. "That's good."

His voice was so flat, hollow, his fingers clawed up to the knuckles into the rocky soil. She wrapped her arms around him gently. "Oh, Shane. I thought you had drowned."

"No. Somehow just the people around me do that."

The pain in his blue eyes was so intense, and she knew it was not the physical kind. "You were with Lonnie when he died, weren't you?" she asked very softly.

He shrugged her off, struggling to his feet, ignoring her helping hands. "I'm the reason he died."

"That can't be true."

He whirled toward her, staggering slightly. "Don't you think I've spent twenty years wishing it wasn't true? Try as hard as I can, but I can't change the facts—not a single one of them." His eyes were wild. "I took him down to the river to look for crawfish. I was thirteen. I told him to stay on the bank, and I waded into the deeper water. The creek was swollen by rain, moving fast. I heard a splash. I turned around."

She watched as his face twisted in agony.

"He was gone. I couldn't find him. No one could find him until hours later."

Kelly took a step toward him. "It was an accident. A horrible accident."

"No, Kelly. I don't buy it. God could have saved him. That's what you believe, isn't it? That's what my brother used to believe, that God is all-powerful, watching over us and protecting us. Isn't that what Christians are taught?"

She opened her mouth to answer, but he cut her off.

"God could have saved Lonnie, even if I couldn't, but He didn't. He didn't save my brother, and that day He let me die, too."

"God didn't take Lonnie to punish you. He loves you."

"Loves me?" Shane's eyes were wild. "Is that love? He destroyed me and my parents. Doctors said Mom died of a stroke six months later, but it was a broken heart that killed her. My father is in a nursing home. He doesn't even know who I am, or what's happening to Todd. I think his mind went because I let Lonnie die."

"No. Your father knows it was an accident."

He shook his head, face drawn into bitter lines. "I lost everything that day, I just didn't know it."

The truth dawned on her, causing her breath to come up short. "That's why you left me, isn't it? You didn't want the responsibility of caring for a child because of what happened to Lonnie."

He reached out to her and then his hands dropped, curling into fists. "I killed my brother. How could I take care of your little boy?" He closed his eyes. "How could I risk it?"

She wanted more than anything to hold him then, to squeeze away the ferocious pain that had built inside him for years. The words from Romans echoed through her memory. *Neither death, nor life...*

A wind blew softly against her face.

Nor things present, nor things to come, nor powers, nor height, nor depth, nor any other created thing...

Shane looked so alone, so completely destroyed.

Shall be able to separate us from the love of God, which is in Christ Jesus our Lord.

"Shane," she whispered, "God hasn't left you. He's put people here who love you, who will stay with you." She swallowed hard, her heart filled to bursting with long-suppressed feelings. "I'll stay, if you want me to."

His eyes rounded, and for a moment the shadow lifted from his face. "All I want..."

She waited, holding her breath.

The hardess returned, covering the light on his face like the cruel rush of waves. "...is to finish this race."

He turned and trudged away down the bank.

"Where are you going?" she called over the water.

"To find my canoe," he said, without looking back.

Shane was the last to finish, but at least he managed that. By the time he found his C-1 bobbing upside down in an eddy, it was past noon. He righted the dented craft and, struggling against dizziness, his battered muscles complaining with every move, he paddled toward the finish point, sticking to the easiest routes.

Chenko helped him drag his canoe up onto the sand. "Well, kid. Sounds like you saved the day. Gwen Falco is going to be all right, thanks to you."

Shane nodded, stripping off his PFD and pulling on a dry shirt Chenko handed him.

"If you don't want to continue, no one would blame you."

Shane located the trailhead, which kicked off the next section of the racecourse. "I'm going to finish what I started."

Chenko nodded. "Good man. I just don't want you dying on me midrace."

"I don't intend to."

"I'll see to it that Kelly takes a look at you when you get to the overnight rest point."

He shrugged. "She's leaving in the morning. She'll probably be gone by the time I get there."

Chenko shrugged. "I think we can talk her out of leaving. Devin's pretty charming when he sets his mind to it."

Shane thought about his last moments with Ackerman. Had he deliberately let Shane go into the rough water? His mind was too addled to know for sure, but he made a mental note to call Bill Cloudman when he returned and make certain that Kelly was leaving Desert Quest.

As he trudged toward the trail, he tried to think through his behavior with Kelly. Why had he shared with her all the trauma from his past? At least she knew now the real reason he'd left her.

And she probably despised him for it. Or worse, felt sorry for him.

God hasn't left you, she'd said.

Then where was He? Shane walked under the thick shade of the trees and felt chilled by much more than his tumble through the water. Todd was on the verge of going to prison. Lonnie was dead. And Kelly would be gone soon.

But she'd offered to stay.

He'd seen the tenderness in her eyes. *I'll stay if you want me to.*

How could he ask her to stay? After he'd hurt her beyond measure? With the danger circling around him? He swallowed. And she now knew that he was responsible for his little brother's drowning.

He slapped at a branch that bobbed in his face.

Finish this leg of the race. Once they were back in camp, he could continue to follow the trail back to the murder at the diner. He felt more and more certain that whoever had murdered the waitress was Olivia's killer. And possibly the reason Rose was on the run.

That killer, he had no doubt, was Devin Ackerman. He'd terrorized Ellen Brown into providing him with an alibi, maybe by poisoning her. He was determined to see Shane disappear.

Good, he thought. All the anger and hurt that he'd shared with Kelly was now forming into a white-hot ball of resolve in his gut.

Ackerman might have tried to drown him. But he hadn't succeeded.

That meant he was getting close. A grim smile twisted his bruised face.

Ready or not, Ackerman, here I come.

In spite of her aching heart, Kelly had returned to find Devin still sitting with Gwen. He jumped up when he saw her approach.

"What happened?"

"I found him. He's okay. He went to find his canoe."

Devin's face must have mirrored the shock in her own. "He's crazy."

She shrugged. Crazy and shouldering more pain than she'd ever realized. How could she not have known the truth? Sensed it? Under his easy smile, his fun-loving nature, he held a burden of guilt that crushed him. She wanted to sit down and cry, to pray for him with all her strength, but she had other duties to attend to.

She checked Gwen over again, monitored her vital signs and wrapped her securely against the chill. The most dangerous thing was shock. They made arrangements for Kelly to drive Gwen to the clinic and for Kelly's replacement to come over as soon as possible to monitor the other racers. Just as she was ready to load a semiconscious Gwen into the car, the woman's eyes snapped open.

She blinked hard and raised a shaking hand to her face. "Am I okay?"

Kelly squeezed her arm. "You're just fine. We'll get you to a hospital so they can check you out fully."

Gwen shook her head. "No. I'm not hurt. I want to go meet Betsy at the rest point."

Devin shook his head. "Oh, no. After what you've been through, you should be off to the hospital, and so should that idiot Matthews. I'm going to call Chenko and see if he's made it there yet." He walked away a few paces and began speaking into his radio.

Kelly crouched next to Gwen, keeping her voice low. "You need to explain something to me."

Gwen's eyes widened. "What?"

"When we pulled you out, you called me Rose."

Gwen's mouth opened and closed.

Kelly stared her full in the face. "You need to tell me how you know my sister."

"Your sister?"

"Listen to me. My sister is in trouble. You know something about that. I want to hear the truth from you right now."

Gwen closed her eyes, and her face grew pale. Kelly reached for her wrist and patted it. "Forgive me, Gwen. I'm sorry to push. I know you've been through a horrifying experience. I'm just worried about Rose, that's all."

Gwen opened her eyes. "I…"

Devin returned. "He made it. Chenko says he looked beat up but okay. He's gone on to the run, and if he doesn't keel over somewhere in the middle, we'll meet him at the checkpoint. I'll help you ladies to the car."

"Gwen is refusing to go to the clinic."

Devin rolled his eyes. "This is getting ridiculous. All right. I guess we can't force you. Kelly, since we've got your replacement on the way, you can personally attend to Gwen for the rest of this leg."

Kelly nodded, and they helped Gwen walk to Kelly's vehicle and slide into the passenger seat. Devin gave Kelly a hug, which lasted a moment too long.

She pulled away. "What's that for?"

"You handled everything so well. Getting help, tending to Gwen, keeping a cool head. I hate to lose you."

"My colleague will do just as well."

He sighed. "No one could replace you, Kelly. I'm going to head back upstream and start the last group. I'll radio you if there's any more trouble."

"Devin?" Kelly asked, stopping him.

"Yeah?"

"What happened when you were pulling Shane in? It seemed like you had him, and then he was sucked back into the water."

Devin's eyes narrowed. "I lost my grip. Water was moving pretty fast. Why?"

"Just wondered."

A cloud passed across the sun, and Devin's eyes glittered in the shadow. "Do you think I let him go on purpose?"

Kelly met his stare head-on. "Did you?"

"No, and I'm going to chalk up your unreasonable accusation to the shock of the incident. Then again, maybe you're starting to buy into Shane's conspiracy theory. Someone tampered with his bike, rifled his trailer."

"You have to admit, those things haven't been explained away."

"Only explanation required is that Shane is a nutcase. I think it's better for you to stay away from him."

"Is that why a snake wound up in my pack? Was that you, trying to make me decide to leave here?"

He blinked. "A snake?"

"Yes."

His eyed danced in thought. "No. I didn't have anything to do with any snake."

She caught a flicker of something on his face that she could not read before he turned away. "See you," he called.

A feeling of unease settled into Kelly's stomach as she got into the driver's seat and headed slowly back up the trail toward the road that would take them to the checkpoint. Devin was definitely hiding something—this time she was sure of it. But at the moment, it was more important to find out more from Gwen.

She adjusted the heater to keep Gwen warm in her wet clothes. Gwen stared out the window.

"All right," Kelly said as they drove. "No more interruptions. How do you know my sister?"

Gwen chewed her lip. "I don't know why I called you Rose. Maybe you misheard me."

Kelly shook her head. "You know my sister. How?"

Gwen stuck a finger in her mouth and chewed on the nail. "I must have heard you talking about her. I got confused, that's all."

Kelly let the silence between them grow while she fought for calm. "Gwen, quit lying to me. I'm not going to stop until you tell me the truth. My uncle is a Tribal Ranger, and I'm sure he could get the local police here to ask you the question if you'd prefer."

Gwen darted a look at Kelly. Then she lowered her gaze to her lap. "I'm a friend of your sister's. We've been friends for years."

Kelly's stomach tightened in excitement. "And?"

"And a year and a half ago she contacted me and asked me to do her a big favor."

"What favor?"

Gwen shook her head. "It sounds crazy when I remember it. She was having trouble staying sober and she had a baby. She couldn't handle it anymore, but she didn't want Charlie to suffer." She shot another look at Kelly. "She brought him to me and asked me to deliver him to you."

Kelly blew out a breath. "So you're the one who left Charlie in my car. That's why you've taken such an interest in him. I thought…" Kelly smiled. "I thought you were a child abductor or something."

"I could have been," Gwen said in a voice so low, Kelly had to lean forward to hear it. "I always wanted a child but, hey, I'm in my mid-forties and I don't even date. There's no baby in my future so when Rose brought Charlie, I begged her to let me keep him." Her eyes filled. "I could have been a good mother to him, but she insisted that he be delivered to you."

There was no malice in Gwen's voice, only sadness.

Kelly was unsure what to say next. "I appreciate your taking such good care of Charlie."

"He's a good boy, and I can tell that you treat him really well."

"I try. Gwen, have you been in contact with my sister?"

"Just a few phone calls here and there."

"When was the last one?"

Gwen shifted in her seat. "Can't remember."

"I think you can. I think there was another reason Rose went on the run. I think it had something to do with what happened at a diner in Ash Ridge. What do you know about that?"

"Nothing."

They drove past eerie rock formations, needlelike against the early afternoon sun.

"You took her baby. She trusted you implicitly. She must have told you why she was leaving. Was it because of the murder of that waitress? She witnessed the crime, didn't she?" Kelly almost gasped out loud as the pieces fell into place. The dark-haired waitress in the photo, the one with her hands over her mouth. "You worked at that diner. I saw your face in a newspaper photo. Did you see who killed that waitress?"

"I didn't see anything. By the time I arrived for my shift, the whole thing was over."

"But Rose saw it. She saw the killer and she's afraid. Did she tell you who it was?"

Gwen seemed to come to some internal decision. "Listen. I know Rose is your sister, but she's my friend. After the murder, she disappeared without a word, and two years later she contacted me about Charlie. She never told me anything except she had to keep Charlie safe and I wasn't to tell anyone anything about her whereabouts. That's all I know.

I brought Charlie to you, and that's all I'm going to say. I don't even know where she is now anyway."

Kelly leaned back in the seat but her mind was racing. Gwen had proved their suspicions correct. Rose could ID Olivia Mason's killer.

The larger question still remained, though.

Who was it?

She had the growing feeling that Rose's life depended on Kelly's finding out the answer.

SIXTEEN

Shane finally stumbled to the rest point sometime after midnight. He skirted clumps of people sprawled out on foam mats, sleeping off their arduous day. He knew he was one of the last finishers, including the final set of canoers who had made their way down the river. The beating he'd taken in the river slowed him. He searched for Ackerman first, determined to confront him about the accident, but he didn't see him. There was a motorcycle parked on the periphery of the lot, the one Devin used to scout out the racecourses, so Shane knew he couldn't be too far away. A couple of vehicles sat in the moonlight. Shane wondered if Kelly's replacement had arrived in one of them.

Groups of people stood chatting, sipping coffee, discussing the final event that would take place at sunup: the spelunking and ropes course. Shane's memory flew back to the beginning of the whole adventure, when he'd pulled Kelly, Charlie and Paddy Paws out of the river. He could still feel her softness in his arms. Moreover, he could picture the mirrored grief in her face when he'd babbled on about Lonnie just a few hours earlier.

How had he lost control enough to spill his deepest anguish, his biggest failure to her? It was a good thing she was leaving.

Somehow his heart did not seem to agree. He made his way toward the medic truck. Kelly was there, talking to an older woman dressed in jeans and a white medic T-shirt. Kelly looked up at his approach, the moonlight painting her face in silvery perfection that made his breath catch.

"Shane. You made it," she said, her smile wide. "Are you okay?"

He nodded, and she introduced her replacement.

"How is Gwen?"

Kelly sighed. "Refusing to go to the hospital until she talks to Betsy."

Kelly introduced her fellow nurse to another racer and walked a few paces away with Shane, quickly telling him what she'd learned from Gwen.

"So she's the connection. No wonder she's been so interested in Charlie. Does she have a way to contact Rose?"

"I haven't been able to get that out of her. Rose made her promise to keep quiet."

They fell into an awkward silence. Kelly looked off into the spangle of stars speckling the horizon. "Anyway, I wanted to tell you…before I left."

He bit back a sigh. "Okay. When are you taking off?"

"At sunup. I'm going to drive back in a few minutes and get Charlie all packed up." She put a hand on his arm. "Uncle Bill and I will keep working on this investigation until we figure out what happened to Rose and Olivia. We won't quit until we do all we can, and maybe it will be enough to get Todd out of jail."

He nodded. "Kell…"

Her eyes roved his face. He felt a pain lancing through him. "Thank you for helping me, and I'm sorry."

She moved closer then, circling him with her arms.

He couldn't resist anymore, but pulled her roughly to

him, burying his face in her hair, holding her tightly to his chest. "I'm sorry that I couldn't be the man you deserved."

She whispered into his ear. "We could try again."

The words sent electric sparks through his body. Try again. Another chance to be with Kelly. Could it be true? Another chance to build a life with the most amazing woman he'd ever known?

He puts people here who love you, who will stay with you.

Shane thought of Charlie, his cheerful smile, his face looking up at Shane with trust.

Just as Lonnie had done.

He could feel the love in her body as he held her. Kelly would give him another chance, and he would be the man in Charlie's life.

What kind of man are you now?

He thought once more of Lonnie, and using all his powers of control, he let go of her.

"You're better off without me, and so is Charlie."

He could see the tears collect in her eyes like chips of diamond in the moonlight. She shook her head and sighed. "I guess I'll go."

He watched her leave and this time, he knew, there would be no second chances. The car pulled away and she was gone, vanished into the darkness as quickly as Lonnie had. Feeling numb and dead inside, he lay down on an empty mat and tried to sleep. As much as his body screamed for rest, it would not come. Finally he got up, thinking a walk might help ease his stiff muscles.

It was quiet around the makeshift camp. Only a few whispers here and there broke the stillness. He caught sight of someone emerging from the tent that served as medical headquarters. It was Gwen Falco, her face drawn.

"Hello, Gwen," he said quietly.

She jumped. "Oh, Shane. You startled me."

"Aren't you supposed to be resting?"

She waved a hand. "I'm fine. I wanted to find Betsy. Have you seen her?"

"No."

She started to say something, then stopped. After a few moments she started again. "You saved my life."

He shrugged. "Happened to be in the right place and all that."

"No. You risked your life for mine. I owe you, and I can see how much you love Kelly so I'm going to tell you something I shouldn't."

"What's that?"

She took a step closer and lowered her voice even more. "I'm glad Kelly's leaving because I'm afraid of what Betsy will do."

"Betsy?"

"She's...unstable." Gwen leaned close. "I think she might have poisoned Ellen Brown last year for getting too close to Devin."

"You think that was Betsy?"

Gwen nodded miserably. "I love my cousin, but she has problems. I've seen the way she looks at Kelly when Devin is close to her."

Shane thought about the snake. "You think Betsy would hurt Kelly?"

"I've already said too much. I just wanted to repay you for what you did for me today."

She turned to go, but he stopped her with a hand on her arm. "You've been helping Rose stay hidden from the man who killed the waitress."

"As I told Kelly, I don't know why Rose ran. All I know is she asked me to deliver Charlie to her sister and I did."

"When did she call you last?"

Gwen shrugged.

Shane stepped closer. "Listen, Gwen. You think you're helping Rose by keeping quiet, but she's in more trouble than she knows."

Gwen shifted slightly. "She called me Thursday from her satellite."

The same day she called Kelly from the pay phone.

"I was about to tell her that Kelly was in camp when she suddenly hung up. I tried to call back many times, but she won't answer. Listen, that's all I know. I've got to go find Betsy."

Shane was startled a second later by Gleeson's rough hand on his shoulder.

"So Rose and Olivia both saw the killer," he said, eyes glittering.

"Eavesdropping? What do you care about Rose and Olivia?"

Gleeson chewed his lip, as if weighing how much to share with Shane. "I never even heard of Olivia until you showed up here at the race, but Rose is another story. I've known about her for a while, but not about her being witness to a crime."

"We need to talk," Shane said, "but right now I've got to call Kelly."

"Afraid Betsy is going to hurt her?"

Shane eyed him. "You were around last year. Do you think Betsy is capable of it?"

"Absolutely. I always thought she had something to do with Ellen Brown's illness."

"Did you tell Ackerman?"

"Yeah. He said I was crazy and I should mind my own business, but when you told me about the snake, I began to wonder if she wasn't up to her old tricks. I've seen the way she's been eyeing Kelly when Devin pays attention to her.

When you told me about the snake, she's the first person I thought of."

Shane's skin prickled. If Betsy truly was unstable enough to poison Ellen…something clicked inside him. It no longer mattered about the race, or his investigations, or even his fear of opening old wounds again. He'd been blessed to share the love of a remarkable woman, even for a short while. Nothing could erase that blessing, and nothing could dull it. The feeling was strange and new, like a secret whispered in his ear.

Nothing could undo what Kelly had accomplished in his heart.

Unless something happened to her.

He fumbled for his phone just in time to see it vibrate, displaying Kelly's number on the screen.

She spoke rapidly before he had a chance to say anything, her words tumbling out so fast he almost didn't understand. Three words came through loud and clear.

"Rose took Charlie? How do you know it was her?"

"I was driving back to camp and I got a call. I don't know the number and the voice was faint. She said it was Rose and she took Charlie to keep him safe. She asked me to meet her at the Spiral Caves. I called the trailer to talk to Aunt Jean and there's no answer."

Shane caught the hint of tears in her voice. "Okay. Calm down. We'll go…"

Gleeson's hand shot out and grabbed the phone, disconnecting the call.

Shane went after Gleeson, who fended him off with a forearm. "Why did you do that?"

Gleeson checked his own phone. "Go talk to her in person. She's about five miles away, headed toward the caves."

"How do you know that?" Shane raised a fist. "Give me my phone or I'll take it from you."

Gleeson braced for a blow, but didn't back down. "I'm trying to help."

"Help? Why should I trust you? You're working for Devin."

"I can't explain it now, but you were right."

"Right about what?"

"The bike. I found the wheel hidden in the brush beside the river. Someone really did score the spokes."

Shane gaped. "But why don't you want me to call Kelly?"

"Because," Gleeson said as he headed away, "it's bugged. So was her old phone, the one that got ruined in the flash flood."

Her phone was bugged? Shane was about to go after him. "Who bugged it?" he called as loud as he dared.

"I did," Gleeson said.

Kelly's body was stiff with fear as she drove. She didn't understand why Shane would hang up. Calling again got no response. She was paralyzed with indecision. She'd struggled with whether she should drive all the way back to camp and find Aunt Jean or continue on toward the caves. It was foolish to drive alone to some isolated location to meet someone who may or may not be her sister, but all Kelly could think about was Charlie.

She reached for her phone to dial the police when she was nearly blinded by a rapidly approaching headlight. It was a motorcycle, and riding it was Shane Mason. Relief surged through her body. He pulled to the side, parked the bike and got in next to her.

"Why did you...?" she started to say.

"Your phone is bugged. Gleeson did it."

Her mouth fell open. "What? Why?"

"I don't know, but I think he was involved in keeping tabs on Rose for Devin. He found my bike wheel, and now he's having second thoughts about his employer. He said he would call the police and meet us at the caves."

"Do you trust him?"

"Not for a minute," Shane said, taking his own phone from its waterproof case and dialing the number of the local sheriff. Afterward he asked Kelly for Uncle Bill's number and called both his home and satellite phone. No answer, so he left messages. For good measure, he removed his GPS unit and tossed it out the window.

"Gwen said Rose called her from her satellite phone and then hung up quickly. My guess is she got a message from Devin. She was afraid to use her phone to contact you again in case he could track the number." Shane's forehead creased in thought. "Hang on. Gleeson said your old phone was bugged too, the one that got ruined."

Kelly felt a cold shiver of fear. "The only time I saw Gleeson before I got here was the day Devin brought him to the clinic. He must have gotten it then." Her eyes widened. "Shane, that means this whole thing—the way I was hired for the race—was all a scam, a way to bring me close to get to my sister."

"How could Devin be sure your sister would come?"

Kelly fought for breath as the stark realization hit her. "Because he'd been listening to our conversations and monitoring our texts. He knew Rose was going to try to see Charlie on his birthday. We spoke about it a couple of weeks back." She gripped the wheel until her knuckles whitened. "Oh no, Shane. I led him right to her. He's going to try to kill her so she can't ID him for the murder of that waitress, just like he killed Olivia."

Shane took her fingers and squeezed. "We won't let him."

"But what if he really does have Charlie?"

He looked at her, deadly determination in his blue eyes. "No one is going to take Charlie away."

She pressed the gas harder. Shane's forehead creased in thought.

"What is it?"

"Are you sure the woman on the phone was Rose?"

"I'm not sure. It was so quick. But maybe she was too afraid to talk for long. She scooped Charlie up and got him away the only way she knew how. My sister has always been impulsive."

"But why wouldn't Aunt Jean tell you that? Have you heard from her?"

Kelly shook her head. "There's no answer at the trailer. I'm so scared."

Shane spoke calmly. "Police are on their way by now. We'll go to the caves and see. If it's Rose, we'll get her to the nearest police station."

"If it's not…" She had to force out the words. "Then someone has abducted Charlie."

He squeezed her fingers. "As I said, no one is going to take Charlie away."

Fear circled in ever-widening waves through her body. Shane tried calling Aunt Jean several more times and got no answer. The police had promised to dispatch a unit to check on her, but Kelly knew the reality. It was a tiny department with many miles to cover. She swallowed hard as the cliffs loomed in the distance. Nestled at the base, shrouded by boulders, was the entrance to the cave where the racers would begin their spelunking the following morning. The whole area was shadowed by the massive corrugated cliffs that rose behind, bathing everything in darkness.

Why would Rose have chosen this spot?

She wouldn't, Kelly told herself. "Do you know the caves?" she asked.

He nodded. "A little. Spent a few hours acclimating there before I tried the ropes. Pull over there, behind those rocks."

She obeyed, and they got out. Shane took a pair of binoculars from the back seat and trained them around the area. "No sign of anyone. We should wait for the police."

"I know." She got out of the car and peered into the darkness, arms wrapped around herself. "But I've got to go."

Shane turned her around. "That's foolish. We know it's likely to be a trap, and the police are on their way."

"I know that, too."

A flicker of light at the mouth of the cave entrance drew both their attention. Shane pulled her back behind the rock. "Lantern?" Shane whispered in her ear.

"I think so."

They continued watching from their place of concealment behind the rock. The light showed again, illuminating two shadows in the opening. Kelly's breath froze. One was the slight figure, which could have been man or woman, but the second was definitely a child.

Charlie.

Her body was electrified, moving on its own now, away from the shelter of rock.

"No," Shane said, pulling her back. "That's what they want. It's a trap."

Tears flowed down her face. "I have to go to Charlie. Right now."

He grabbed her face and held it between his palms. "I won't let you get hurt." His lips suddenly brushed hers, igniting tingles through her body.

"This is about my sister, Shane. You shouldn't be putting your life on the line."

He sighed, staring into her eyes. "Remember when you told me that God loves me?"

She nodded, afraid to answer.

"I'm not sure I believe it, but I know your love came from someplace special. I'm not deserving of it and I didn't do anything to earn it, so maybe that really is a God thing. I know I threw that away when I left, but I'm not leaving now. Not anymore. I'm here and we're going to get through this together."

He kissed her, and his mouth on hers pushed away a corner of the terror that threatened to drown her.

God help us, Kelly prayed as she took Shane's hand and they walked toward the flicker of light.

SEVENTEEN

Shane felt as though his senses were heightened with Kelly's soft fingers clasped in his, the cool breeze washing over his face, the crunch of gravel underfoot. Something inside him was changing too, blowing through him like the crisp wind that pushed the clouds away until the sky was brilliant and clean. He did not allow himself to wonder about the determination he felt surging through his body. He marched closer to the cave, all the while planning escape routes if Ackerman showed his hand.

And he would. There was no doubt in Shane's mind that it was a trap. His goal was to play for time, to keep Charlie and Kelly safe until the police arrived.

I don't know how we're going to do this, but we're going to make it.

He realized with a jolt that he was speaking not to himself, but to God. It made no sense.

He shook his head to clear it, just as they crept around the last massive boulder separating them from the mouth of the cave. The cave opening was nothing more than a yawning black circle against the cliff face, until the lantern light was held aloft.

It was definitely a woman. The darkness made it impossible to see her face, but her hair was long and dark, her figure slight. Next to her, holding her hand, was a child. Shane's heart leapt to his throat. He'd hoped it was a ruse, a trick of the light, but the little voice that wavered through the night was real.

"Mama Kelly?" Charlie called.

"Charlie," Kelly cried, the words sounding torn out of her.

"Come closer," the woman said, and Shane identified her immediately.

They reluctantly moved forward a few paces, Shane keeping Kelly a step behind him.

Shane decided to take control of the situation as best he could. "Betsy, enough with the theatrics. Why did you bring Charlie here?"

She laughed. "I don't have to answer that. My job was to get Kelly here, and that's what I did. Too bad you came along too, Shane, but I guess that's all for the best. Come in."

"No. You send Charlie out."

She gave an impatient sigh. "That's not how it's going to work."

"Mama Kelly?" Charlie whimpered. "Owww, you're squeezing my fingers too tight."

Kelly bolted forward. "Get away from him."

"Come on in, Kelly, and you can have him."

Shane put out a hand to stop her, but it was too late. Kelly ran toward the cave. He followed as quickly as he could. Kelly moved into the circle of light and snatched Charlie. The boy tumbled into her arms, crying.

She patted his back and murmured comforting words into his ear. "It's okay, honey. I'm here now."

"That's better," Betsy said. "Finally, you're behaving properly. You should never have come here, throwing yourself at Devin. The snake should have convinced you to go. What kind of mother keeps her kid in a place with snakes?"

"You're crazy," Kelly whispered.

As far as Shane could tell, there was no weapon in Betsy's hand. What was her game? Was Ackerman hiding in the shadows?

"Kelly is leaving," he said. "There's no need for all this. She planned to go in the morning. You didn't need to go to all the trouble."

"Oh, she's definitely going now," Betsy said. "You, too."

Kelly hissed at her. "What did you do to Aunt Jean?"

"The old girl is fast asleep. I dropped a little sedative into her chili pot this morning while she and the kid were out for their morning walk. She'll be out like a light for a while. Guess Charlie doesn't like chili because he put up a good fight when I snatched him after I finished the race."

Kelly looked at her in horror. "You did this because you thought Devin had feelings for me?"

"Devin has feelings for lots of women," she hissed, "especially the pretty ones."

"Betsy," Shane said, keeping his voice calm, trying to soothe Betsy's rage. "What's really going on here? You didn't go to all this trouble, taking Charlie and luring us here, just to get Kelly out of your way."

"So true," a low voice said. "It was a mutually beneficial arrangement."

Shane gaped as Martin Chenko stepped into the pool of light, a hard hat on his head.

Chenko laughed. "The look on your faces is just priceless."

Shane suddenly realized the full extent of his miscalculation as he took in the gun clasped in Chenko's hand. He almost groaned out loud. "Gleeson was working for you.

He was tracking Rose, and he brought Kelly into the race under your direction."

Kelly gasped. "Mr. Chenko? You've been after Rose all along? It wasn't Devin?"

"Of course not," Betsy snapped. "Devin would never get involved in anything like that."

"You're the one who killed that waitress," Shane said to the man who had morphed from race producer to multiple murderer in the passing of a few moments.

Chenko sighed. "Things got out of hand. I was asking her about Rose, if she'd seen her in town. I knew I was close. Unfortunately, my temper got the better of me. The irony is, I was right. Rose was close—closer than I thought. She saw me running away."

"So did my sister-in-law, Olivia Mason."

"I had no intention of hurting Olivia until I happened to cross paths with her when we brought the race here last year. We'd arranged with her husband to borrow some horses. I saw her watching me, and I knew it was just a matter of time before she put it together, even though I had a beard and my hair was different. I had no choice. It was easy to shoot her; your brother was passed out drunk. I killed her, put the gun in his hand and fired again."

"To make sure he had gunshot residue on his fingers."

"It's the details that really make a plan come together," Chenko said matter-of-factly. "When I found out who you were, I tampered with the bike and tossed that rock at you, but still I find you here in the middle of this mess."

Shane gritted his teeth. "My brother is in jail for murdering her."

Chenko cocked his head. "I'm sorry about that. It was the easiest way out. Please hand over your phone now, Mr. Mason."

Shane reluctantly tossed it to Chenko, who deftly grabbed

it and put it in his pocket before he turned to Kelly. "None of this would have happened if your sister hadn't run off with my child."

Kelly pulled Charlie closer. "Charlie."

"Yes. I gave her everything, took care of her, helped her get sober, and then when she was finished using me, after getting pregnant with my child, she took off." His eyes rounded. "How is that right? How is it right for her to deprive me of being a father to my flesh and blood? I had a right to find her and my boy." He cast a loving glance at Charlie. "He's a good boy, isn't he? I think I can see my mother in him, around the eyes."

Shane edged closer. All he needed was a little distraction. Cops were on their way.

Just keep the gun away from Kelly and Charlie.

"All I want," Chenko said, "is Charlie and Rose."

Kelly stood and pushed Charlie behind her. "You're going to kill my sister," she breathed. "She's the only one left who can ID you for the murder of that waitress."

Chenko waved the gun impatiently. "I'm a businessman. I look for the most efficient solution to any problem. Enough dillydallying. We're on a tight time line here. Take out your phone and dial your sister's satellite. She has it on at the moment and she's close, maybe on her way to snatch Charlie and make him disappear again."

"How do you know where she is?"

He clucked like a disapproving grandmother. "So naive."

"Gleeson?" Shane asked.

"He thought he was helping me find my wife and child. His ex took away his access to his child, too, so he understands the injustice."

"But you neglected to tell him you killed a woman, and you're going to do the same thing to Rose," Shane said.

"It's not important what I did or did not tell him. Gleeson

downloaded software onto the phone I gave Kelly. We've been tracking her calls. Rose must have suspected it, because she stopped calling, didn't she? That might have been my fault. I sent a generic text to see if she'd respond. That spooked her, I think. My error for trying to rush things, but when I feared you were leaving, it created a sense of urgency."

Kelly looked down without answering.

"Doesn't matter. We're using a GPS tracker. All you need is a target phone number. The last time she sent you a text, we harvested her satellite phone number and installed the tracker. Her GPS pings back to my computer as soon as she powers up her satellite, and there you go. Instant play-by-play. As soon as she contacts you again, we've got her."

"You have no right," Kelly said, her voice trembling with rage.

"And she had no right to take my child."

The chill in his words unsettled Shane even more than the gun.

"We can come to some sort of agreement," Shane started to say, playing for a few more precious minutes.

Chenko shook his head. "We don't have time for this. I'm sure you called the police before you came, so they are no doubt on their way. Text your sister and tell her to meet us at the abandoned mine at the top of Red Bluff. We'll take care of our business there. She's still checking her messages, I'm sure, even if she isn't calling you."

"I won't do it," Kelly said, her face stricken.

Chenko moved quickly. Before Shane could react, he edged closer and pressed the gun to Shane's temple. "I think you will, or this man will die."

"Don't do it, Kelly," Shane said, anger thundering in his veins. "He's using me to bully you into betraying your sister."

The anguish on Kelly's face was clear.

"Shane…" she whispered.

He tried to communicate with his eyes. *You and Charlie are the most important people in my life and I love you both.* "Don't give him what he wants, Kell."

"Doesn't really matter anyway," Chenko said. "If you don't send it, I will. This will just keep your friend here alive for a few more minutes, maybe prevent the child from watching someone shot down in cold blood." He kept the gun pressed to Shane's temple.

Kelly's eyes slid from Chenko's face to Shane's.

"It's going to be okay, Kell," Shane said. The police would be there soon. Or maybe Gleeson would turn up to help.

With shaking fingers, and tears streaming down her face, she texted the message.

"Very good. Now we will get out of here before the police arrive. Besides," he laughed, "the racers will be here at sunup. We've got to get Betsy back by dawn. She may actually win this thing after all."

Betsy smiled happily. "He's promised me a spot on the race staff."

"How cozy," Shane said. "Think Devin will still want you when he finds out what you've been up to?"

Her smile dimmed, eyes narrowing into slits. "He's never going to find out."

Shane felt again the surge of determination. Somehow, some way, Shane would make sure he did.

Chenko gestured with the gun toward the back of the cave, and Shane suppressed a groan. Of course Chenko wouldn't take them out the front; there might be cops waiting. Chenko knew the cave intimately because he'd scouted it for the race. He would know how to get out without being seen.

He saw the look of fear flash across Kelly's face as Betsy pushed her toward the rear of the cave. "Where...?" she began.

"Time to do a little spelunking," Chenko said, snapping on the headlamp and prodding them into the darkness.

The cave passage was slick with moisture, the temperature considerably cooler than the air outside. Kelly shivered, holding tight to Charlie's hand.

"An even fifty-eight degrees, no matter the weather," Chenko said from behind her. "I admire that constancy. Inspires me in my daily life."

Kelly thought *relentless* was more appropriate. "You don't even love my sister. Why not let her go? She won't tell anyone; she'll stay quiet to keep Charlie safe." The word *safe* bounced up to the flat ceiling and down again, Betsy's lantern light winking off the thousands of tooth-shaped formations on the walls, like tiny jaws waiting to chew them up.

"We had an agreement, a business arrangement if you will. I cared for her, supported her, and in exchange she was to stay with me and our future children, too."

"Things change," Kelly heard Shane say. "You can't own people or force them to love you."

"A verbal contract is binding in this case," Chenko said, his words sibilant, like a living thing in the darkness.

"I want to go back to the trailer," Charlie said.

Kelly put an arm around him and helped him through the passage, which narrowed ahead. The air smelled of unopened places, secret tunnels and chasms that spidered out around them. The cold seeped into her bones, chilling her to the core.

"Don't worry, Charlie, my man," Chenko said. "We're

going to have lots of fun together as soon as we say good-bye to your real mother."

Charlie gave her a questioning look and she forced a smile. "It's going to be okay, sweetie."

Inside, Kelly fought panic. Chenko would take Charlie and hide him somewhere they'd never find him.

Oh, God, help me. Help me, please.

Chenko's tone turned cheerful. "It was a stroke of luck, your coming to work at the clinic. Gleeson had been keeping tabs on you for quite some time at my request. I arranged with him to fake an injury, and Devin took him over. You were so eager to take the job."

She felt like a fool. In her eagerness, she'd delivered Charlie and Rose into Chenko's hands.

They continued on, slower now as the passage wound in lazy zigzags further into the darkness. At one point they walked across a path that dropped into a deep crevice on one side, and she held on to Charlie's shoulders and pushed him in front of her, holding tightly to him. Then the way widened out, the floor bristling with hard rock formations that resembled little trees. She stumbled once and felt Shane's hand on her arm, helping her up and giving her a comforting squeeze. She felt a surge of guilt at dragging him into the situation. He should have stayed outside, gone for help.

A thought sickened her. The moment he had seen Chenko's face, Shane became a liability, too. He would kill them along with Rose, and Charlie would be raised by this monstrous man. Her mind raced, trying to come up with some sort of escape plan, but there was only darkness pressing in from every side. Even if she could break away, she could not escape the rocky labyrinth, not with Charlie, and Chenko would kill Shane without a moment's remorse.

They entered a soaring chamber with stalactites feathering down like graceful fingers. Betsy held the lantern higher, but the light hardly pierced the darkness. In the center of the chamber was an irregular platform of rock, sparks of crystal gleaming where the light hit them.

"Is it diamonds?" Charlie asked.

Chenko laughed. "No, son, that's..."

He didn't have a chance to finish his sentence. A figure appeared at the top of the rock. Everyone froze.

Gleeson's silver hair shone in the gloom. "Chenko, it's all over. "

"Why, Mr. Gleeson," Chenko said genially. "My loyal employee. Come to help?"

"I'm not your employee anymore. I worked for you because I thought you had a right to find your son. I didn't know that killing his mother was part of the bargain. You neglected to mention that you'd killed that waitress and Shane's sister-in-law."

"Suddenly grown a conscience? You didn't mind prying into the life of this young man here, spying on Kelly, or bugging a few phones. Now you've got objections?"

Gleeson shifted enough that Kelly could see the outline of a gun in his hand. He shook his head in disgust. "I should have figured it out when you sabotaged Shane's bike. You were trying to keep him out of the picture while you reeled Rose in like a fish on the line."

Kelly felt Shane stiffen beside her, moving slightly closer to her as if he could protect her from what was to come. Gleeson lifted the gun higher. "I don't want to shoot anybody, so don't make me do it. Let's walk out of here like civilized people."

All eyes were riveted on Chenko. Kelly didn't notice Betsy's hand in motion until it was too late. She hurled a rock through the air. Gleeson's attention was drawn instinctively toward the missile, giving Chenko the split second he needed.

He fired three times in rapid succession. There was a scream and Betsy dropped the lantern, which rolled behind a ridge of rock, blotting out the light.

Kelly felt Shane pulling her to the floor as she heard bullets ricocheting through the cavern, pinging against the rocks with thunderous sound. Something sharp scraped her cheek, but she didn't care. She reached for Charlie to pull him under her, but his hand was suddenly yanked out of hers and she heard his squeal of fear.

"Charlie!" she screamed over the sound of shouting and running feet. Someone moved around her and then Betsy's light was restored, Shane's grim face suddenly illuminated as he held up the lantern.

Kelly sat up, heart pounding. Betsy lay on her side, blood leaking from her shoulder.

Gleeson emerged from where he'd taken cover behind a rock. He was also bleeding from a wound on the temple, where a bullet must have grazed him. He knelt next to Betsy. "She got caught by a ricochet. Doesn't look too bad."

Kelly was on her feet, scanning wildly. She locked eyes with Shane. The truth nearly squeezed her heart to a stop.

Chenko was gone.

And so was Charlie.

EIGHTEEN

Shane took the flashlight Gleeson removed from his back pocket. "I took one of the motorcycles from camp. It's hidden in the bushes. I'll stay here with Betsy and wait for the police."

"Sure you're okay?"

Gleeson grimaced. "More mad that I bought Chenko's lies than anything." He looked down at Betsy, whose face shone with fury and pain. "She'll be all right. Get going."

Shane nodded, handing Gleeson the lantern, already turning to run down the corridor.

Kelly was next to him in a flash.

"Stay here with Gleeson," Shane told her.

"I'm going with you."

"You'll be safer here."

Her eyes blazed. "If you leave without me, I'll crawl through the dark on my hands and knees after you."

He'd seen that ferocious determination in her face before, and he smiled in spite of himself. She grabbed a handful of his jacket and followed behind as they moved quickly down the passage he believed Chenko had taken. They could not be that far ahead, and Chenko had Charlie to tote along so there was a good chance they could catch him.

Pushing as fast as they could, they scanned ahead as far

as they could see for any glimpse of Chenko's headlamp. Before them the tunnel lightened, the darkness fading to gray as they approached an exit. They plunged out into the predawn as another volley of gunshots broke the silence, slamming into the cliff face behind them. Shane rolled on top of Kelly, carrying them both behind a nearby pile of rocks.

Chenko did not wait to fire any more shots. They heard the sound of a motor gunning. Shane poked his head out in time to see a white pickup careening out into the darkness. "Text your sister, quickly."

Kelly cried out. "My phone. I dropped it when the shooting started back there."

"Too late to go back. We might not find it anyway. Let's go."

He found the motorcycle and kick-started it. Kelly clung to his back as the bike surged along. As soon as he could, he peeled off on a side road.

"Where are you going?"

"Someplace where we can watch for your sister. We have to get to her before Chenko does."

Kelly held on tighter as they rose along the path that paralleled the highway. The going was steep in some places, twisty in others. Shane prayed he had chosen the right way. He had only spent a day of exploring the area when he'd first arrived.

The path cut along the top of the cliffs until it dropped down behind some grass-covered hills. "Hold on!" he yelled back to Kelly as he took them off the trail. They bumped and jostled their way to an overlook where they could see the road below. Chenko's pickup crept along steadily, toward the mouth of the abandoned mine.

Shane turned off the headlight and cut the motor. Shane and Kelly watched as Chenko eased the pickup down a gentle slope in the road that took him out of view. Kelly's fingers dug into his arm. "Charlie," she whispered.

He didn't have a chance to respond. The moment he'd been hoping for arrived. Far down at the base of the cliffs where they had started their journey, a gleam of headlights glowed. He pointed. "Look there."

"Is it Rose?" Kelly breathed.

"I think so." Shane got off the bike and turned to face Kelly, who dismounted after him, her eyes filled with fear.

"Listen, Kelly, I know I've let you down, but I think I've got a way to get Charlie and Rose to safety." He was afraid to ask the question. "Do you…can you trust me?"

She blinked and looked away.

His heart sank.

Then suddenly she threw her arms around him and squeezed him tight. "Yes, Shane. I trust you."

He clasped her close, burying his face in her hair, pressing his lips to her neck. After a long moment that was too short, he pulled away, and emotion pounded through his heart with a force he hadn't felt before.

He's put people here who love you, who will stay with you.

He realized in a moment of clarity that Kelly and Charlie were the people God had sent.

In spite of the past. In spite of Lonnie's death. Because he was loved.

His throat thickened as he felt Kelly's arms around him. And he had what it would take to save them.

"This is what you need to do," he said.

Kelly found herself reseated on the back of the bike, clinging to Shane as he careened back down the trail in the direction from which they'd come.

Did she trust Shane?

He had broken her heart so thoroughly she thought it would never mend, yet here she was, holding tight to the man she could not erase from her life. She was surprised to find that she no longer wanted to. She pressed her cheek to his back and felt his heart beating, felt the new life that seemed to course through his soul. Something had changed in him, and she only hoped they would live long enough for her to find out what it was.

Shane turned the bike down a steep path that left Kelly breathless, and when he reached the main road, Rose's car was a half mile in front of them.

Rose. Kelly's heart leapt.

All this time she'd been waiting and fearing that each precious phone call or text from her sister would be the last one. Picturing her drunk and suffering at the hands of those who would take advantage.

Like Chenko, who believed he owned Rose.

She tried to tamp down the terror she felt when she thought of Charlie there alone, scared, with a father he'd never even met, a father who had set a trap to kill his mother.

Hang on, Charlie. We're coming.

Shane pushed the bike faster until they were within fifty yards of Rose. All of a sudden, Rose's small car zoomed ahead.

Shane pursued, but Rose kept up her frantic pace.

"She thinks we're after her!" Shane shouted.

Kelly had to clutch Shane tightly to keep from being unseated as the chase continued.

Stop, Rose, Kelly pleaded silently.

But Rose continued to accelerate until she swerved and crossed the narrow road. Her tires lost traction and the car spun, coming to rest against the red cliff. In a moment, Rose was out of the car, running madly up the road.

"Stop!" Shane called, bringing the bike to a screeching halt. "We're here to help you."

But Rose kept on, stumbling and tripping, regaining her footing and running awkwardly along the road. Shane jumped off the bike and pursued her, Kelly at his feet.

Rose had no chance against Shane's long legs, and he caught up with her in a matter of moments, finally grabbing hold of her arm until she tumbled to the ground.

Still she came up fighting, pushing and smacking him for all she was worth.

"Rose!" Kelly yelled. "Rose, stop it. He's trying to help you."

She continued to fight until Kelly hollered again. "Stop it, sis. You're fighting the wrong people."

Kelly's voice must have finally penetrated her sister's consciousness because Rose jerked and went still. Shane held her arms for a moment longer.

"I'm sorry to tackle you," he said.

Rose's glance went from Shane to Kelly. Suddenly a brilliant smile lit her face. "So he's the guy with eyes so blue they could melt your heart?"

Kelly's face grew hot. "Never mind that," she said, helping her sister up and ignoring Shane's amused glance. She took a long look at her wild twin. Rose's hair was bedraggled, her clothes worn. She'd lost so much weight since Kelly had seen her last, and her eyes were sunken, but she was sober.

Kelly felt tears sliding down her face, and she clasped her sister in a tight embrace.

"I'm sorry, sis," Rose said. "I'm so sorry. I should have gone to the police long ago, but I was scared he'd take Charlie." Her face crumpled. "And now he has."

Kelly squeezed her. "We'll get him back."

Rose shook her head. "He wants me dead, and he won't

stop until I am. My only hope is he'll give Charlie back to you if I hand myself over."

"No," Kelly said. "He's not going to kill you or take Charlie."

Rose sniffled and wiped a hand over her face. "It's funny. I was born two minutes before you and that makes me the big sister, but you're always trying to fix my sorry life."

The look of utter despair on Rose's face almost made Kelly start crying again, but Shane put a hand on both of their shoulders. "I'm sorry to intrude, but we've got to move or Chenko will get suspicious, since he's tracking your progress."

Rose's eyebrows shot up. "I worried he was listening to my calls somehow; that's why I stopped calling from my satellite. I didn't realize he could use it to check my location."

Shane nodded. "Right now I'm hoping he thinks you're stopping to get your bearings. We've got to move. I have a plan to make this work, but it's going to take luck."

Kelly shook her head. "Not luck." She pointed her finger to the skies. "Help."

Shane's face spread into a slow smile, so tender it took her breath away. "A whole lot of help," he agreed.

Shane turned off the motorcycle headlight and hung back just far enough behind the small car that he would not be seen, he hoped. It felt wrong, all wrong to send the two women off alone to face a killer, but he knew it was their only option. The only way it would work was if Charlie was safely out of harm's way.

All right. Help is what I need here. I don't know where You and I stand, and I've got a lot of questions, but...

He took a deep breath, summoned more courage than he'd ever felt before, and offered up a prayer.

I need You to help me, Lord.

And that was as much as he could manage. He still felt the shadows of grief, regret and even guilt, but the anger had somehow slipped away.

As they began the final climb that would take them to meet Chenko, Shane dropped farther behind, watching the woman he loved drive slowly into the trap of a madman.

Kelly's fingers gripped the steering wheel so hard they started to cramp. All the while, Rose kept shaking her head. "I had no idea you were working at the race. With him. I saw the picture in town and it freaked me out. How could he be so close? I decided to run, get away to someplace safe and hide for a while. I thought you were working in the hospital."

"You should have checked in more often. Come to visit, the way you said you would." Kelly regretted her words as soon as she said them.

Rose looked away. "I know. I didn't want you and Charlie or Uncle Bill to see me…"

Her words trailed off, but Kelly knew the rest. Drunk. The addiction still had its hooks into Rose.

Kelly reached out a hand, and clutched her sister's. "We'll get you help. You can beat it, but not if you run away."

Rose sniffed. "I've tried so hard but the booze always wins."

"Not this time," Kelly said, praying they would get the chance to see her words come true. They pulled to a stop just at the crest of the slope, as Shane directed. It was peppered with shrubs and clusters of rocks. Kelly hoped it would be enough to hide them for the few seconds they would need.

Shane killed the motor and pulled the motorcycle into the shadows. He watched with his heart in his throat as Rose's car stopped at the top of the slope. In his mind he pictured the topography. The road sloped down toward a flat area at the bottom where the mine entrance lay, barred to prevent unwanted visitors. Both sides of the road were lined with trees and shrubs. Chenko would have driven the pickup to the flat area and parked, waiting patiently for his victim to arrive.

He knew Chenko had been watching, pinpointing Rose's location the entire time. What was he thinking now, as he knew the woman he'd been chasing for four years was within his grasp? He could practically feel the hatred that coursed off the man, hatred born of loss and rejection. Shane thought how close he'd come to letting his own grief and anger poison his life.

He listened intently for the sound of approaching vehicles. Nothing.

There was no sign of any police presence, and he hadn't really expected there to be. Unless they'd found Gleeson already, there was no way for the authorities to know where Chenko had demanded that Rose meet him. It was clever. Shane imagined that Chenko had a new identity and funds waiting, meticulous businessman that he was. He would walk away from the race, perhaps with the prize money in his possession, and melt into a new life.

He moved his bike into position, at the top of the slope behind a screen of bushes. He saw Chenko poke his head around the edge of his pickup, cautious. His white face shone like a beacon in the darkness.

Shane could not see his face, but he imagined the smug expression.

You're mine now. After all these years.

He thought about Kelly. She'd just gotten her sister back, and he was not about to watch Rose ripped away from her now.

"Come on," Shane breathed. "Just move a little more. Show me that you've got Charlie somewhere safe."

Chenko sidled out from behind the truck, and Shane felt a surge of elation. Charlie wasn't with him. He'd locked him in the car. Imprisoned, like a coveted trophy locked in a case.

All right, Chenko. It's time.

Shane saw Rose's car stop for a moment behind the screen of foliage before it began moving slowly down the slope.

Shane stared at Chenko until his eyes burned.

Keep looking at the car.

Chenko moved out further now, his gun ready in his hand. "Thanks for coming, Rose," he called. "I've been waiting for this moment for a long time." His laughter was filled with exultation. "You should have stayed with me. We could have been a family—you, me and Charlie. But now…" He held up his hands in a gesture of helplessness. "Now I'm going to have to raise my boy alone."

The car crunched along the gentle slope, gaining some momentum.

Chenko leveled the gun at the driver's side.

Gut tightening, Shane hoped the darkness would be enough.

"Stop the car, Rose, and get out."

The car moved more quickly, tires kicking up bits of gravel as it went.

"Doesn't matter if you stop or not," Chenko called. "I'm killing you one way or another. Wouldn't you rather stop and do this privately?"

The car rolled on.

"All right!" Chenko shouted, his face twisted in rage. "Have it your way."

He began to fire the weapon.

* * *

Kelly screamed at the sound of exploding glass. She pulled Rose to the ground next to her, peering out from the shrubs, grateful they'd crept from the car just before it started its downward roll toward Chenko.

She wanted to leap from behind the bushes and find Shane, but she had another mission.

Get Charlie.

Grabbing Rose's hand, the two of them made their way quickly to the end of the shrub line. There was no more substantial cover, only low-lying foliage that wouldn't conceal them for long. Kelly held up an index finger. "Wait," she mouthed.

Her sister's face was ghastly pale, the eyes half-wild, but she did as Kelly commanded.

When Chenko fired the next shot they ran, hurtling down the road as fast as they could before they dove behind the pickup, scuttling around to the side, facing away from Chenko.

Kelly frantically yanked on the door handle but found it locked. Chenko wasn't taking any chances.

She risked standing and peeking inside. Charlie was curled in a ball, lying on his side, eyes shut. The window of the old truck was unrolled only about an inch, not enough for her to get her hand inside.

Her body was electrified. Any moment, Chenko might turn from the car and spot them yanking on the truck door.

She flattened herself to the ground and looked under the truck. The empty car was slowing now, coming to a stop at the flat area near the mine entrance, windows shattered. Chenko warily moved closer. He would discover their ruse and find them in the act of trying to steal Charlie.

Rose searched in the dirt, hands scrambling wildly. "We've got to find a rock."

She found a sharp chunk of granite and brought it over her head to smash the window.

Kelly grabbed her hands. "No, the glass might hurt Charlie. Let me try."

She stood shakily and pressed her mouth to the opening in the window. "Charlie, honey, it's Mama Kelly. I need you to open the door so we can go home, okay?"

Charlie whimpered, but did not move.

Rose shook her head. "He's too scared. We have to break it."

"No," Kelly hissed. "Too much noise." She tried again. "Charlie, you're such a big man, aren't you? Shane is going to help us get home, and he promised you could ride on the motorcycle, but you've got to open the door right now, okay? I'm going to take you home, back to Paddy Paws."

Heart in her throat, Kelly watched as Charlie uncurled himself and reached his little hand toward the lock.

Time seemed to stand still as Charlie pulled, and Kelly thought he might not have the fine motor skills to do it, but finally, after a long moment of agony, she heard the lock slide open.

She eased the door open and Charlie leaped into her arms. Her heart nearly burst at the relief she felt to have the child safe in her embrace.

The relief did not last long. Chenko made it to the car and peered inside.

He let out a roar of rage and spun back toward the truck.

NINETEEN

Shane was close enough to read Chenko's body language. The moment he discovered their ruse, he reared back in a murderous rage. He would go toward the truck.

Not if Shane could help it.

He kick-started the motorcycle and roared down the slope before the car rolled to a complete stop. Chenko's attention was distracted just long enough. Shane was coming quickly upon him before he realized what was happening. He fired wildly as the motorcycle leapt into his line of vision, the shot whistling by Shane's face. Ducking down as much as he could and zigzagging the bike, he kept after Chenko.

The man's face creased in fury as he fired again, the shot slamming into the rocks. Shane read it in his eyes. Chenko weighed the satisfaction of killing Shane against the prize he really wanted. He spun on his heel and sprinted down-hill toward the truck.

Gritting his teeth, Shane hit the gas and flew top speed at Chenko. Had Kelly gotten Charlie out?

The look on Chenko's face was pure rage. He might just hurt Charlie to prove a point, if he realized he was on the losing end of the deal. Shane pressed harder and pulled within feet of Chenko as he neared the truck. Chenko raised his gun hand to fire toward the vehicle, and Shane knew he had to put a stop to the deadly game.

He accelerated, came alongside Chenko and leaped off the motorcycle.

They came down in a tangle of limbs.

The gun went off again before Shane rolled on top of Chenko, slamming his hand into the ground until his grip failed and the gun skittered away. Chenko aimed a punch at Shane that landed on his jaw, stunning him, but Shane's grip on Chenko did not weaken.

Somewhere in the back of his mind, he heard sirens approaching, but still he did not let go of Chenko.

Chenko's face was mottled and sweaty. "You can't take what's mine," he spat.

Shane stared into the mad eyes. "They were never yours, and they never will be."

Uniformed officers suddenly appeared and secured Chenko, taking him into custody and helping Shane to his feet.

"So I guess I finally got the answer to my question," a deep voice said.

Shane was surprised to see Bill Cloudman in Tribal Ranger uniform, a slight smile on his lips.

"What question was that, sir?"

"The one about what kind of man you are." He jerked a thumb at Chenko. "I just caught the end of your crazy stunt, and now I know."

Though it was dark, Shane thought he caught the barest glint of admiration on Bill's face.

"Did you find Jean?"

He nodded. "She's okay. Resting back in the trailer. Refused to go to the hospital. Stubborn."

Shane smiled. "Runs in the family?"

"Not just in my family, I guess."

Bill smiled, or maybe it was a trick of the moonlight. Shane didn't have time to ponder, as Kelly ran toward him, throwing her arms around him. Bill melted into the background. Shane embraced her tightly. "Charlie?"

"He's okay. Scared but not hurt." She pulled away to look him over closely. "Were you hit? You're bleeding."

He shrugged. "I think I caught some glass."

She nodded, then started to cry, tears streaming down her face. "How can I thank you for what you did? How can I ever thank you?"

He pulled her to him and kissed her, his lips tingling and sweet emotion flowing through him. "I should be thanking you."

"Why?" She half laughed. "You nearly got killed tonight trying to help my sister and Charlie."

"Because you reminded me that what I have is more important than what I've lost."

Her eyes met his, glittering like fallen stars in the darkness. He kissed her again.

It was dawn by the time they made it back to the base camp. Aunt Jean greeted them with massive, tearful hugs. "I'm so sorry," she cried. "I let that woman take Charlie. How could I have allowed it?"

Kelly reassured her aunt as best she could. "There's no way you could have known. No way any of us could have known."

Shane patted her on the back as they sat at the battered table, sipping mugs of coffee. Charlie had finally been soothed enough to go to sleep, Paddy Paws curled up next to him. The trauma he had endured made Kelly cringe inside, but with the help of Aunt Jean and Uncle Bill, he would overcome it.

And Rose, Kelly thought with a start. Rose was back for

her son. Kelly's stomach clenched, and a helpless feeling surged through her. Charlie would go back with his real mother. Why did it feel as if a part of her would go with him?

She looked at Shane. He was bruised and dirty, but he looked more peaceful than she'd ever seen him. Where would they go from here? He would return to his hometown, help clear his brother of Olivia's murder, and then what?

Her thoughts were interrupted by a knock at the door. Kelly opened it to find Devin and Gwen on the doorstep. She ushered them in. Rose went immediately to embrace her friend.

Devin's cheeks were red, his easy confidence evaporated. "I know I'm intruding. I just wanted to make sure you were okay and tell you how sorry I am."

Shane cleared his throat. "Maybe I should be apologizing. All this time, I thought you were the one responsible for killing Olivia."

Ackerman blanched. "Me? Of course wasn't me." He stopped and sighed. "I do have some blame in all this. I knew Betsy was irrational sometimes. I even had suspicions that she had something to do with making Ellen Brown sick, but I never did anything about it. Maybe if I had, or if I could have seen Chenko for what he was…"

Kelly touched him on the shoulder. "There's no way to go back and undo things. Betsy didn't get the chance to hurt anyone else."

"And she's never going to have the chance again," Uncle Bill said. "Neither will Chenko."

Ackerman nodded. "Anyway, I told the racers what happened. Most have already left. I can't refund their money so I guess the race is officially finished." He gave them a final nod and left.

Gwen shuffled forward, put a cardboard box on the table and turned to follow him.

"What is it, Gwen?"

"A cake. For Charlie's birthday. I made it yesterday."

Rose hugged her friend, and Kelly saw tears in Gwen's eyes. "Thank you for everything you've done for Charlie," Rose said.

Gwen shrugged. "I'd do anything for him."

Kelly stood. "We're leaving soon for Uncle Bill's house. It's a couple of hours from here. We're going to have a little party Monday, just like we planned. Why don't you come, too? You can ride back with Rose, and we'll find someplace for you to sleep."

Gwen shook her head. "No. It's a family thing."

Kelly's voice shook a little. "Gwen, you tried your best to take care of Charlie by bringing him to me, and you did your best for Rose. That makes you family. Please come."

Gwen's face contorted and, for a moment, Kelly thought she would decline. Then she nodded. Rose wrapped her in a hug, and there was sniffling all around. Then Rose turned to her family. "I need to say something, too. I've made so many bad choices, and I can't believe I almost lost Charlie for good." She wiped away a tear. "I'm not strong enough, not yet. Aunt Jean is going to help me get into treatment. There's an eight-month program and then some outpatient care. I wanted to…" She looked at Kelly. "I need to ask if you'll take care of Charlie for me. He thinks of you as his mother anyway." Her gaze dropped to the floor.

Kelly took her sister's hand. "I will look out for Charlie as long as he lives, and I'll make a home for him until his mother comes back, for good this time."

The sisters embraced until both of them had cried themselves out. Aunt Jean made sandwiches for everyone and after they'd eaten, Uncle Bill and Rose began to pack up for the drive home while Aunt Jean and Gwen swept the floor. Kelly cleaned the kitchen and when she looked up, Shane was gone.

Her heart sank.

What they'd been through, the new feelings she'd sensed in him, had been fleeting after all. Things would return to the status quo. She was angry at herself for thinking otherwise. He'd asked her to leave the race, and now that it was over, they would part ways.

A tap at the window startled her.

Outside, Shane crooked his finger at her. Wiping her hands on her apron, she excused herself and went outside, dreading the final goodbye she knew was coming.

"Hey," she said.

"Hey, yourself. You okay?"

She nodded, breathing deeply to maintain a calm tone. "Now that Charlie and Rose are safe, I'm just fine. How about you? Have you contacted your brother?"

"I spoke with his lawyer. We're going to meet Monday morning and go over the details."

She smiled at the look of satisfaction on his face. "I'm so happy for you and Todd."

"Me, too. How are you doing with the return of the prodigal sister?"

"I'm glad Rose is going to take some time and work hard on her sobriety. It's the best thing for Charlie."

"Is it the best thing for you?"

She shrugged, picking at a loose thread on her shirt. "I'm glad I can take care of Charlie for a while longer."

He stared at her, the rising sun gilding his hair, his eyes that piercing blue tint that colored her dreams.

After a moment's hesitation he said, "Charlie is blessed to have you."

"Blessed? I'm surprised to hear you use that word."

"I'm surprised to find myself saying it." He looked away for a moment. "I learned some things about myself out here, because of you."

She saw emotion shimmering on his face, underneath his breezy tone. "What did you learn, Shane?"

"I'm a real slow study, but I finally figured out that God put a woman in my life to show me the truth, to help me find out what kind of a man I am."

She looked at him in wonder. "What kind is that?"

"A man who loves you more than anyone he's ever met or ever will meet."

Her throat thickened, and she fought tears. "Thank you for saying that, but I know you don't want to be involved in raising a child, and now I understand why. You did so much for me, for us, and I understand you need to move on."

He started to speak but she stopped him.

"Please, let's make this quick and easy for both of us."

"Okay," he said, suddenly pulling her into his arms. "Quick and easy. I don't understand all this God stuff. I've spent my whole life raging at him for taking my brother. Now I see that He doesn't hate me because He brought you into my life. And Charlie, too. I'll probably always worry about taking care of a child, and there's plenty I don't understand, Kell, but one thing I've got down crystal clear. I love you, I love Charlie and I'm going to work every day from now on to convince you that I'm the kind of man you can trust this time."

Her pulse pounded. "You are?"

"Oh yes." He pressed his lips to her temple and traced them across her forehead.

Tears flooded her eyes, trickling down her face. She gripped his arms, steadying herself against the onslaught of emotion. "Shane, I can't take losing you again."

"I'm here to stay. I promise." His arms tightened around

hers. "And someday, when you're ready," his lips moved to her ear and whispered, "I'm going to convince you to marry me."

She could hardly form the words. "Oh, yeah? Sounds pretty cocky, Mr. Mason. What makes you so sure I'll say yes?"

He looked into her eyes, his own flashing in the morning light. "I've been told my baby blues can melt a woman's heart. Who could resist that?"

"Not this girl," she whispered. Heart soaring and joyful laughter bubbling up inside, she pulled his lips to hers.

* * * * *

Dear Reader,

Shane is caught up in the race of his life. The odds are stacked against him, and he is nearly overwhelmed by both internal and external challenges. His greatest obstacle is the crippling guilt he feels over the death of his younger brother.

We all run our own races, don't we, dear reader? Personally, I sometimes feel overwhelmed by my own burdens along the way. There are so many things weighing us down—guilt, failure, physical pain, sickness—but we strive to finish, knowing that the only way to complete the challenge is with His help. It's the ultimate comfort, knowing that no matter what we face, God is there to help, forgive, listen, and most of all, to save.

Whatever race you're running today, I hope you will feel Him empowering you to tackle the journey. "For I am convinced that neither death, nor life, nor angels, nor principalities, nor things present, nor things to come, nor powers, nor height, nor depth, nor any other created thing, will be able to separate us from the love of God, which is in Christ Jesus our Lord." Romans 8:38–9

I always treasure hearing from my readers. Please feel free to contact me via my website, www.danamentink.com.

With love,

Dana Mentink

QUESTIONS FOR DISCUSSION

1. Kelly raises her sister's child while Rose grapples with alcoholism. How do you think Kelly feels toward her sister at the beginning of the story?

2. Kelly and Rose's mother was a drug addict for most of their lives. How do you suppose Kelly escaped a life of addiction?

3. Endurance racers have qualities that enable them to overcome brutal physical obstacles. What kind of mentality does it take to participate in an event like Desert Quest?

4. When Todd is falsely accused of murdering his wife, his faith begins to falter. What Bible passage would you suggest to help him overcome his doubt?

5. Charlie has grown up without his mother. If you were Kelly, how would you explain his mother's situation to him?

6. Shane enjoys racing because it gives him the fleeting sense that he is in control of his life. In what ways do we nourish similar feelings?

7. The river is a metaphor for our own personal journeys, which can be both a thrilling ride and a tragic experience. How can we ensure that the trip is a worthwhile adventure?

8. What are your thoughts about Betsy Falco? Why do you think she developed into the kind of person she is at the end of the story?

9. Gwen had no children of her own, though she longed to keep Charlie. How can Gwen cope with the fact that God denied her request to be a mother?

10. Chenko believes Rose used and abandoned him. How should he have dealt with the situation for his own sake and Charlie's?

11. What do you think of Gleeson? What kind of person is he?

12. Shane learns things about himself and his relationship with God. How do you think he's changed?

13. What do you imagine the future will hold for Kelly and Shane?

INSPIRATIONAL

Wholesome romances that touch the heart and soul.

SUSPENSE

COMING NEXT MONTH
AVAILABLE FEBRUARY 14, 2012

DANGEROUS IMPOSTOR
Falsely Accused
Virginia Smith

THE ROOKIE'S ASSIGNMENT
Fitzgerald Bay
Valerie Hansen

PROTECTING THE PRINCESS
Reclaiming the Crown
Rachelle McCalla

SHATTERED IDENTITY
Sandra Robbins

Look for these and other Love Inspired books wherever books are sold, including most bookstores, supermarkets, discount stores and drugstores.   LISCNM0112

REQUEST YOUR FREE BOOKS!

2 FREE RIVETING INSPIRATIONAL NOVELS
PLUS 2 FREE MYSTERY GIFTS

YES! Please send me 2 FREE Love Inspired® Suspense novels and my 2 FREE mystery gifts (gifts are worth about $10). After receiving them, if I don't wish to receive any more books, I can return the shipping statement marked "cancel". If I don't cancel, I will receive 4 brand-new novels every month and be billed just $4.49 per book in the U.S. or $4.99 per book in Canada. That's a saving of at least 22% off the cover price. It's quite a bargain! Shipping and handling is just 50¢ per book in the U.S. and 75¢ per book in Canada.* I understand that accepting the 2 free books and gifts places me under no obligation to buy anything. I can always return a shipment and cancel at any time. Even if I never buy another book, the two free books and gifts are mine to keep forever.

123/323 IDN FEHR

Name	(PLEASE PRINT)	
Address		Apt. #
City	State/Prov.	Zip/Postal Code

Signature (if under 18, a parent or guardian must sign)

Mail to the **Reader Service:**
IN U.S.A.: P.O. Box 1867, Buffalo, NY 14240-1867
IN CANADA: P.O. Box 609, Fort Erie, Ontario L2A 5X3

Not valid for current subscribers to Love Inspired Suspense books.

**Are you a subscriber to Love Inspired Suspense
and want to receive the larger-print edition?
Call 1-800-873-8635 or visit www.ReaderService.com.**

* Terms and prices subject to change without notice. Prices do not include applicable taxes. Sales tax applicable in N.Y. Canadian residents will be charged applicable taxes. Offer not valid in Quebec. This offer is limited to one order per household. All orders subject to credit approval. Credit or debit balances in a customer's account(s) may be offset by any other outstanding balance owed by or to the customer. Please allow 4 to 6 weeks for delivery. Offer available while quantities last.

Your Privacy—The Reader Service is committed to protecting your privacy. Our Privacy Policy is available online at www.ReaderService.com or upon request from the Reader Service.

We make a portion of our mailing list available to reputable third parties that offer products we believe may interest you. If you prefer that we not exchange your name with third parties, or if you wish to clarify or modify your communication preferences, please visit us at www.ReaderService.com/consumerschoice or write to us at Reader Service Preference Service, P.O. Box 9062, Buffalo, NY 14269. Include your complete name and address.

LISUS11B

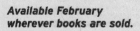

celebrating
15 YEARS

Love Inspired®

SUSPENSE

RIVETING INSPIRATIONAL ROMANCE

Law enforcement
in Fitzgerald Bay is full
of Fitzgeralds raising
speculation that they may be
tampering an investigation
to protect one of their own.
Internal affairs detective
Nick Delfino is sent
undercover to investigate
the powerful clan. But the
deeper he digs, the more
he comes to admire them...
especially his rookie partner
Keira Fitzgerald.

THE ROOKIE'S ASSIGNMENT

by VALERIE HANSEN

FITZGERALD BAY

*Available February
wherever books are sold.*

www.LoveInspiredBooks.com

LIS44477